HOT JOCKS 4

CROSSING
THE LINE

New York Times & *USA Today* Bestselling Author
KENDALL RYAN

Crossing the Line

Copyright © 2020 Kendall Ryan

Developmental Editing by

Rachel Brookes

Content Editing by

Elaine York

Copy Editing by

Pam Berehulke

Cover Design and Formatting by

Uplifting Author Services

ABOUT THE BOOK

Recovering from a pulled groin muscle isn't exactly how I planned to spend my much-needed summer vacation.

But I'll admit, being nursed back to health by my gorgeous friend Bailey, who's just graduated from medical school, doesn't exactly sound like a hardship.

We spend a week together at my family's beach house, a week of swimming and barbecues, a week of entertaining my little cousins and sleeping right across the hall from each other. A week of watching Bailey grow closer with my mom and sisters, and my wacky but lovable grandma. A week of enjoying Bailey tending to me—which is saying something, because it involves a lot of shoving ice packs into my underwear and taping up sore muscles.

She's funny and kind, and after just being myself for the first time in a long time, I find my walls come tumbling down. But when Bailey says she's not looking for a relationship, I'm bound and determined to be more than just the fun hookup who sprained his groin a second time—this time with her.

PLAYLIST

"Electricity" by Silk City, Dua Lipa

"Sexy Boy" by Air

"One More Night" by Maroon 5

"Jealous" by Chromeo

"Body" by Loud Luxury featuring Brando

"What's Luv?" by Fat Joe featuring Ashanti

"Connection" by OneRepublic

"Till I Found You" by Phil Wickham

CHAPTER ONE

Truth Bombs

Asher

I see it. I want it. I take it.

Hockey career. Fancy apartment in Seattle. Women. It doesn't matter what, it's just how I've always operated. Unapologetically and without shame.

Only not now. Because right now, everything is totally screwed.

"Are you okay?" Owen asks, peering over the rim of his pint glass at me. He's our team's goalie and one of my best friends.

With a sigh, I give him a noncommittal shrug. I'm getting really tired of everyone asking me that.

I'm nursing a pretty serious injury. A concussion that will keep me sidelined for the rest of the season, and a pulled groin that makes everything painful—walking, sitting, never mind something more vigorous like sex. That's completely off the table.

I'm sitting in a dimly lit bar around the corner from my apartment with two of my teammates while an ice water sweats in front of me. It feels like a metaphor for my life right now. We spent the day getting fitted for tuxedos for Owen's upcoming wedding, where we'll all be groomsmen. Then we grabbed a bite to eat and lingered after our plates had been cleared away for one more beer for them—and water for me.

Leaning back in my chair, I push one hand through my hair. "Who the hell knows? Maybe this was meant to happen. Maybe it was the universe telling me I've been going too hard for too long, and I needed a break before I burned myself out completely."

Even as I say the words, I doubt there's any truth to them. I just don't think my teammates want to hear how fucking depressing it is that I won't be playing with them.

"Damn, Asher. That's some poetic shit right there," Teddy says. Like me, he's one of the team's starting centers.

"Eh." I tilt my head. "Even a blind squirrel finds a nut once in a while."

The guys chuckle.

"Speaking of nuts . . ." Owen gives his eyebrows a wiggle, and we all fall into easy laughter.

There's the Owen we know and love. You never know what's going to come flying out of his mouth. Like the time we were detained at the airport by security after the TSA agent asked him, "Sir, do you have any weapons or explosives on you?"

"You mean other than this bomb-ass dick in my pants?" Owen said with a smirk.

That little comment cost us over an hour in a special interview room.

Good times.

He's a little unpredictable. A little wild. That's not to say he hasn't chilled out some since becoming engaged earlier this year. He has. But he's still very much Owen, which means providing regular comic relief to our group of friends, often in the way of dirty jokes and clever one-liners.

Teddy is a little older, a little more levelheaded of the two, and can generally be relied on for providing solid advice. Only right now, I don't want to hear anyone's advice about what I should be doing with my unexpected and unwanted time off.

Before the guys can probe any further, we spot a couple of our female friends across the bar—and my stomach tightens. Bailey is petite and gorgeous and as smart as a whip. She's about to graduate from medical school, and though I've never admitted it before, I have a major thing for her. She's with her friend Aubree, who's dark-haired and a little quieter and more serious. I've been friends with both of them for the past few years after meeting them through mutual friends.

Even if I wanted to, I can't help the way my gaze skims over Bailey's curves as I watch her approach. A fitted pair of blue jeans artfully torn at both knees encase her legs, a black T-shirt hugs her chest, and white tennis shoes complete her casual yet sexy-as-fuck look. Her blonde wavy hair skims the tops of her shoulders, accentuating the long, delicate column of her neck as her inquisitive brown eyes lock with mine.

I grab my water and take a long drink, trying to douse the strange tightness in my chest as she and Aubree stop beside our table.

"Hi Asher," Bailey says, meeting my eyes with a soft smile.

"Hey," I rasp out, suddenly feeling a little dizzy.

"What are you two ladies up to tonight?" Teddy asks with a grin.

Bailey tucks a strand of honey-colored hair behind her ear, meeting my gaze briefly again before looking away. "Just picking up a takeout order. We're staying in tonight, but had a sudden craving for truffle fries and stuffed mushrooms."

I nod. It's what I'd wanted to do too—stay in, that is. "Sounds like fun."

"How are you feeling, Ashe?" Bailey asks, looking at me with concern.

Who knows, maybe it's her medical training taking over, but something feels different about her expression. I look fine from the outside—no black eyes, bandages, or bruises. But she's smart enough to know that the deepest wounds are sometimes the ones you can't see.

"I'm out for at least two weeks, maybe the rest of the season." I can't help the hint of frustration in my voice.

The details of my injury have been plastered all over the news, the replay shown in slow motion on TV so many times, it felt like I was watching it happen to someone else. But the pain in my crotch and the fuzzy feeling inside my head serve as constant reminders that it was me who was slammed into the boards that game.

Bailey gives me a concerned look. "I'm sorry to hear that."

"That's awful," Aubree adds, her mouth turned down.

I don't like the look of pity on everyone's faces when I tell them. It's one of the reasons I haven't been responding to text messages or phone calls— I don't want to hear anyone's disappointment that I'm not playing in the playoffs. It's only the biggest moment of my life, and now it's happening without me.

"You guys want to take a seat while you wait?" I make a move from the stool I'm occupying but Bailey shakes her head.

"I'm good," Aubree adds.

"I'm actually going to visit the ladies room before we go," Bailey says.

This bar is great—it's dark, quiet and relaxed, but one weird thing is that the restrooms are located out back, in a separate building beside the parking lot. And since there's no way I'm going to let Bailey wander out there alone after dark, I rise from my seat. "I have to go too. I'll walk with you."

She nods and leads the way toward the back exit.

I know I shouldn't, but I can't help myself from checking out her ass her she walks. *Jesus, Asher.* When we reach the door, I hold it open and Bailey slips past me. The scent of her floral shampoo is like a sucker punch to the nervous system. I'm suddenly all keyed-up and I don't even know why. Since I lied about needing to use the bathroom, I enter the men's room and wash my hands, then wait for her outside on the dimly lit sidewalk.

I haven't spent much one-one-onetime with Bailey, but I didn't need to in order to know she was good people. A med-school student well on her way to becoming a doctor. Kind eyes. A little sassy. Curves for days. Exactly what I'd look for in a woman. Not that I have to go looking these days. The past few years have been an all you can eat buffet of girls eager for my company. Not that I've complained. Hell no. Far from it. But that doesn't mean I might feel differently if I ever had the chance with a good girl like Bailey.

Footsteps announce her arrival. "Thanks, Ashe," she says when she spots me leaning against the concrete wall. Her small smile signals that the jig is up. She knows I only came so she wouldn't come back here alone.

"Anytime." Our eyes meet for a second longer than necessary and yet, I can't make my feet move. "Having a good summer so far?" I ask.

She nods. "It's been a little busy, but yes." Bailey shifts, shoving one slender hand in the pocket of her jeans.

Memories of last summer flash through my brain. One long weekend we'd all taken a ferry to Orcas Island to stay in a couple of cabins located right along the rocky shoreline. We'd gone whale watching and had visited a winery. I think Elise and Aubree had planned the whole thing, but I honestly don't even know. I'd chipped in some money for the cabin and for groceries and packed a rain jacket and my hiking boots. That was the weekend I'd first started noticing things about Bailey that I never had before. Like how smart she was, how fun, and how pretty she was— even without a drop of makeup, or access to a blow-dryer, she had all my attention.

Not that she really noticed me. Hell, if she noticed I was a single dude at all, she didn't let on. She'd mostly hung out with the girls. She's close with Sara, Elise, Becca and Aubree. And I mostly hung out with the guys—all the usual suspects from the team were there. But still, Bailey and I crossed paths at the breakfast table and at the nightly bonfires. I secretly loved how she gave zero fucks about wearing sweatpants and cozy fleece sweaters all weekend long. How she cursed when she burnt her hot dog in the fire and made one of the guys switch with her.

With the twitch of smile, Bailey continues past me, leading the way back to the table, and the spell is broken.

When we reach our group, the topic of discussion is summer travel.

"So, you're going to the big family reunion now?" Owen asks me, bringing me back into the conversation.

"No," I grumble.

"What family reunion?" Teddy says before taking another sip of his beer.

Clearing my throat, I lean forward, putting my elbows on the table. "It's my grandma's eighty-fifth birthday this summer, and she wanted all the family to get together at her house on the beach in San Diego. It's next weekend, so I assumed I wouldn't be able to go, that we'd still be in the playoffs. And you guys will," I say, giving my teammates a stern look, "but I won't."

Owen makes a confused expression. "So, why not go? Coach will let you."

"I'm not going because the team says I have to bring a nurse with me, and that's fucking ridiculous. I'm a grown-ass man. I'm not going to spend my vacation getting sponge-bathed by some stranger, or being frowned at any time I try to have a beer. I'd rather keep my ass home. At least then I can relax in my own space."

"A trip to California for a week?" Bailey asks. I find myself nodding as I meet her eyes again. "I'll do it," she says, causing all of us to appraise her with varying degrees of confusion.

"Huh?"

"Be your nurse. I'll do it. I'll come with you." Her wide brown eyes meet mine in earnest.

"Why?" I blink at her, still utterly confused.

She shrugs. "I don't know. A free trip to San Diego?"

"You're a doctor, not a nurse."

"True. But I have two weeks off before my residency starts."

I can barely hear the rest of her words. Suddenly, everyone's got an opinion, and they're all encouraging this—loudly.

"Do it, dude," Owen says, then finishes off his beer with a long swallow. "It'll be much better than the team assigning you some stranger, and you'll get to see your family. That has to improve your sour-ass mood, man."

He's right, but I kind of wanted to dig my heels in on this one and stay home, holed up like a miserable bastard. I know already that it will be difficult to maintain my sour mood once the California sunshine hits my skin, or when my grandmother dishes out one of her inappropriate stories.

If I stay home, I'll only be punishing myself. And Bailey looking so excited by the idea of this trip has me a little intrigued.

"Okay. I'll clear it with the team next week. Our head athletic trainer may want to talk with you first."

Bailey nods, still smiling. "Sounds good. Keep

me posted."

"Will do." My heart rate kicks up at the possibility of heading to SoCal with Bailey.

After a few more minutes of small talk, the girls excuse themselves to pick up their order, which is ready, and then it's just us guys again.

"Be careful with Bailey," Owen says after a tense minute of silence.

"What the hell is that supposed to mean?"

He gives me a pointed look. "It means that you're *you*, and she's *her*, and I'm just trying to keep it real. She'll be doing you a favor traveling with you, remember that."

"I'm not following, dude. I understand she'd be doing me a favor." Even as I grumble out these words, I know what he's referring to.

For years, I've played hard and rested little in my time off. I've gone from game to game, play to play, fight to fight, like an addict constantly looking for his next fix. Hockey is the only thing that makes me feel whole, and I've pursued it relentlessly. Of course, now that's all off the table. At least, for the time being.

When my parents first divorced, I was young

and hurt, filled with a rage that no amount of hockey could drown out. I would launch myself at opponents, fists flying, without always knowing the reasons why.

It was a behavior that got rewarded. My coaches loved it. But now I see it was a defense mechanism. I never had to think. Never had to feel. I just acted. I did what felt good and what came naturally to me—and that was hockey. Except now I can't play. At least, not right now, and it feels like some kind of prison sentence.

A lot has changed over the last decade. I'd like to think I've matured, calmed down a bit. But my reputation, it seems, hasn't faded.

The rumors about me are vicious. People say I'm selfish. An asshole. Some of it is true. Maybe more than some of it. But I don't care to admit that to myself right now, because more than just my ego was bruised.

"Bailey's a big girl. She can handle herself." Teddy studies me as if he's trying to read my intentions.

My only intentions are to visit with my grandmother and try not to focus on the fact I've been temporarily sidelined from doing the one thing I love.

"Just wanted to put my two cents in," Owen says defensively, leaning back with his bulky forearms crossed over his chest.

Even though I've played it off, I know exactly what Owen's saying. My reputation for playing a tough game of hockey is one thing, but there's also been a lot of women. More than a few.

When Bailey shows up in her bikini at the beach looking like a snack, will I have enough willpower to resist? It's a question I don't seem to have an answer to.

I guess time will tell, and I'll find out when we reach San Diego.

But there's one thing I already know.

For the first time since my injury, I feel like a weight has been lifted off my shoulders, and it's because of the pretty blonde with the gorgeous brown eyes.

CHAPTER TWO

Balancing Act

Bailey

Balance and I have always had a rocky relationship.

Figuratively, I am the queen of balance. Being
in med school is one giant balancing act. I always
have a thousand things to get done at once, which
has made me the master of the to-do list and a god-
dess when it comes to prioritizing.

But literal balance, as it turns out? I'm not so
great at that. A little fact that must have slipped my
mind the other night when, between handfuls of
truffle fries, I agreed to join Aubree for yoga this
morning.

As I dig my toes into my mat, trying to "center
my breath" as our instructor calmly recommends,
I watch Aubree out of the corner of my eye. She's

bending and stretching like a rubber band in her light pink sports bra and matching leggings. She makes it look so easy, like someone pulled her straight off a fitness influencer's Instagram account. When I try to match her stance, bringing one foot to the inside of the other thigh, I wobble like I've had one too many shots of tequila, and eventually fall.

This is so not my definition of self-care. In fact, after four years of med school, that term has pretty much been struck from my vocabulary. But when I do relax, my version of taking care of myself looks a lot more like last night, wearing comfy clothes and enjoying some comfort food while doing absolutely nothing, definitely not any form of exercise. But Aubree insisted yoga would help relieve some of my med-school tension, and would do a few favors for the back pain and bad posture I've developed from four years of being hunched over books and my laptop.

"Half-moon pose, open up your heart chakra."

Our teeny blond-haired instructor has a voice like honey, making her instructions sound more like polite suggestions. Which is a good thing, because my half moon looks more like a quarter moon, and I'm fairly certain there is no medical proof of a chakra, heart or otherwise.

At the end of our final flow, when everyone closes their eyes and bows to the front of the studio, I take the opportunity to adjust my leggings and fix my current wedgie situation.

Yeah, like I said. Not much of a yogi. But I made it through my first-ever yoga class without sustaining any permanent injuries, so I'll count it as a victory.

"So, what did you think?" Aubree asks, her tone optimistic as she grabs a spray bottle of sanitizer and starts spritzing down her mat.

"I think I need to work on my balance before I come back," I say with a laugh. *Understatement of the year*. "But it felt good to stretch. I've been dealing with some serious strain in my supraspinatus."

Aubree rolls her big honey-colored eyes while simultaneously rolling her yoga mat into a compact purple burrito. "English, please."

"Sorry. Some pain in my rotator cuff."

Shoving her mat under her arm, Aubree hops to her feet and extends one hand to me. "Hi, Bailey. Have we met? I'm Aubree. I work in the nonprofit world. You're going to have to come out of science land for a second here and speak in normal people language, not doctor language."

I laugh as I readjust the hair that's slipped out of my ponytail. "My shoulder hurts, and I'm glad we did yoga to stretch it out. Better?"

Her mouth quirks into a smile. "Much better. Now, come on. Let's grab lattes to go before you have to launch back into science land again at your meeting with the team doctor."

A bubble of nervousness builds in my gut. Is a stomach chakra a thing? Because if so, mine is definitely out of whack.

I still can't believe I volunteered to go on this trip with Asher and his family. I should have kept my mouth shut—I can see that now. But to be fair, keeping my mouth shut was never a strength of mine. Small talk. Bold promises. Gossip. Those are all things I excel at. Being docile and silent isn't a strength I've ever possessed. My mouth has gotten me in and out of trouble plenty of times over the years. Heck, it's what landed me in this yoga class this morning. And now, it has volunteered me to serve as Asher's personal nurse in San Diego for a week.

One more slipup, and I'm investing in a muzzle

for myself.

Our favorite coffee shop is just around the block from the yoga studio. The second Aubree and I walk in, a familiar barista nods my way and starts prepping my usual order, a large vanilla latte.

"I guess you're officially a regular," Aubree says over her shoulder as she steps up to the counter, ordering herself a cold brew.

By the time I'm up, the barista already has my latte waiting for me, steam billowing from the lid. Extra hot, just how I like it.

"Your usual blueberry muffin, Bailey?" he asks, already reaching into the pastry case.

Jeez, am I really that predictable? I guess I have been spending a lot of time studying here lately.

I suck in a deep breath, realizing that, yes, apparently, I am that predictable. Do I *need* a snack? Maybe not. But do I want one? Most definitely. It takes about five seconds for me to cave.

"Yeah, why not?" I shrug. "I deserve it."

"So, this meeting," Aubree says, working on the perfect balance of sweetener in her cold brew. "Is there a non-sciencey way for you to tell me what it's going to be like?"

I shrug, testing the first sip of my latte. It's just barely cool enough to avoid burning my tongue. Perfection.

"I don't totally know," I say with a shrug. "But I'm sure they'll give me the lowdown on what kind of treatment Asher has been receiving, anything I need to look out for, or medications he needs to take. All the good stuff."

Aubree nods along, her ponytail bobbing enthusiastically with her head. "Sounds simple enough."

Yes, it probably would be if my patient weren't our super-hot friend Asher.

"Let's hope it is."

Aubree's brows knit together as she takes a long, thoughtful sip of cold brew. "Which are you most excited about? Playing doctor, or the unbelievable free vacay-in-the-sun part? Or the extended-time-with-Asher part?"

"Is it wrong if I say all of the above?"

My response surprises Aubree as much as it does me.

Yes, I'm pumped about the doctor stuff and the vitamin D I'll be soaking up. But in all the daydreaming about lying on the beach and being trusted to serve as a real medical professional, I almost forgot about the part where I'll be one-on-one with Asher Reed for a week. The guy is hot as sin, there's no denying that.

"It's not like anything will happen," I assure her as we head for our respective cars. "I mean, he's injured. And . . ."

"And?" Aubree asks. "Is there an 'and'?"

I pop a bite of muffin into my mouth to avoid admitting that no, there isn't an "and." In my dream scenario I'd be all over him before our plane was cleared for takeoff. Not that I think he thinks of me like that. But, hey, a girl can dream.

"I wouldn't be going on this trip as his friend who just so happens to think he's drool-worthy," I remind her. "I would be going as his *nurse*."

It's a reminder for me too. The team would be trusting me with the health of one of their star centers. There's no way I could let them down. If this crazy idea is approved, that is.

Once Aubree and I say our good-byes, I head home and change into something a bit more professional. Then it's a quick drive to the Ice Hawks' training facility.

Inside, I'm greeted by security and asked for my ID. Then I'm directed down the hall to the third door on the right. The hallways are polished gleaming concrete, and on the walls are murals of players, both those on the current roster and legends of the past, along with sayings in block letters like **NEVER STOP PUSHING** and **FAILURE ISN'T AN OPTION**.

When I walk into the training room, a man who must be the team's athletic trainer is reviewing paperwork on a clipboard while Asher sits nearby on an exercise ball, one leg bouncing and fidgeting impatiently. He's dressed in a pair of black athletic shorts and a worn-looking green Ice Hawks T-shirt, his ash-blond hair barely poking out from beneath a backward Ice Hawks cap.

I take another step forward and the trainer spots me from over his clipboard and extends his hand to me.

"You must be Bailey Erickson."

I take a few steps forward and extend one hand. "And you must be the guy I'm here to see." I shake his hand firmly and return his smile.

"Trey Donovan, MS, ATC." He returns my handshake with a firm grip while rattling off those letters behind his name.

I'm actually pleased with myself that I know what they stand for. He's not a doctor but has a master's degree in science and is a certified athletic trainer. I'm sure he studied sports medicine in grad school. He's wearing khakis and a green polo imprinted with the team's logo and bright red tennis shoes, and he looks friendly enough, gazing at me from over the clipboard he's still holding.

"I understand you've completed your clinical rotations and are waiting for your residency to begin," he says.

I nod, not the least bit surprised that they had me checked out. "Yes. I'll be an internist at William Simmons starting in July."

"And you know Mr. Reed already, I understand."

Trey nods toward Asher, who stops fidgeting for a moment to shoot me one of his famous smiles. The nerves in my stomach take flight, and I'm left feeling a little jittery.

"What's up, Bailey?" Asher lifts his chin at me, then flashes me another smile that makes my heart pound a little faster.

I give him a cautious smile back, trying not to get lost in those gorgeous blue eyes.

"Hop on up here," Trey says to Asher, patting a black padded table, then turns back to me. "We're dealing with a pretty standard-issue concussion, so—"

"No contact sports, and lots of water and rest," I say, finishing his sentence.

An impressed smile twitches across Trey's lips. "Exactly right. His balance is another thing we're keeping an eye on. It may have been compromised."

I nod, watching him. "I'll monitor that."

Trey hands me the results of Asher's recent CT scan to look over, but I admit this isn't my area of expertise, and he walks me through it. I'm relieved to hear it's not too serious, but they're treating it cautiously with plenty of rest, and he won't be cleared to play again until all the symptoms subside, like the headaches and dizziness. Makes sense.

Asher takes a seat on the table, but Trey pats it again. "Lay back, would ya?"

Inhaling slowly through his nostrils like he's

slightly frustrated, Asher lies back, extending his legs in front of him. It's a little strange to be standing beside an exam table with Asher laid out before me, but I keep my focus on Trey.

"There's one other injury we need to keep an eye on," Trey says, motioning to Asher's medical charts on the clipboard. "Mr. Reed sustained a grade-two groin strain when he fell. So he should avoid vigorous activity at all costs."

My gaze involuntarily flicks down to Asher, who is wearing a smug grin on his face. I pray to God that Trey doesn't notice that I'm starting to blush. Of course, it has to be a groin injury. Of all things. Which means my attention will have to be focused on this freakishly handsome man's junk. I'm so screwed.

"Right," I mutter, collecting myself. "So, plenty of rest and ice on his adductor. Right leg?"

"Correct. I'll show you what to look out for. Asher, would you prop your leg up on the table, please?"

Asher does as he's told, and Trey gestures for me to see for myself. Cue me gulping down the enormous lump in my throat.

Sure. No problem. I'm just going to grope Asher

Reed's crotch for a second. For medical purposes.
And I'm not going to have any dirty thoughts in the
process.

I approach Asher hesitantly, looking for any signs that this is as inappropriate as it feels, but he gives me none. *Duh.* Because this is a medical exam, not a come-on. I need to keep my mind out of the gutter.

Leaning over him, and with the gentlest touch I can manage, I push the leg of Asher's basketball shorts up his thigh. The fabric is loose-fitting, so it slides out of the way easily. He's wearing black boxer briefs, and from beneath the edge of them, I can see the start of a bruise.

"May I?" I ask, my voice a little shaky.

He nods, and I carefully move the fabric aside, trying to ignore how much I like the feeling of my fingers on his skin. But that feeling is quickly chased away when I see the swelling and deep purple bruising high up on his inner thigh. *Ouch times ten.*

"Jeez, Ashe," I murmur softly, my fingers absently stroking the tender spot.

"Yeah, trust me, I know," he says, his voice deep and husky.

My attention is pulled away when I realize Trey is talking again.

"I see a lot of injuries like this. It's just the nature of playing hockey—lots of groin and hip injuries. They use their glutes when they skate, and when those muscles tire, the hip flexors and groin muscles get overused."

I can't let my mind wander to Asher's glutes, because *sweet baby Jesus* . . . the ass on this man. Hockey butt—it's a thing and it's glorious. Google it.

"I'll show you how I like to tape it before you leave," Trey says, "and I printed out a sheet of stretches and strengthening exercises you can make sure he does every day."

I nod. "Any pain medication I should be aware of?" I ask while Asher sits up. I'm assuming the answer is yes. With this amount of swelling, I imagine that even walking must be incredibly painful for him.

Trey snorts. "Good luck. He has a prescription, but he's adamant about not using it."

"That's because I don't need it." Asher scoffs, tugging his shorts back into place to cover his bruises. "I'm not a pussy."

I roll my eyes and rise back to my feet. "No, but you are an injured player. And what I say goes, Asher. So if I think you need the meds, you're going to take them."

Asher snickers as he adjusts his Ice Hawks cap and goes back to bouncing his leg. "Yes, ma'am."

"By *ma'am*, I'm assuming you mean MD," I snap, planting one hand on my hip. "And stop fidgeting your injured leg. That looks like vigorous activity to me."

Trey chuckles, interrupting our little spat. "It seems like you've got a good handle on Mr. Reed's condition. Just don't let him give you too much of a hard time this week, Bailey."

"Not a chance," I say, giving him a half smile and another firm handshake. "Rest assured that Asher is in good hands."

Good hands that, frankly, I'm going to have a hard time keeping off of my patient.

CHAPTER THREE

It's Go Time

Asher

"This is it. No turning back now," I say, shifting to look at Bailey, who's seated next to me. The flight attendant has just made an announcement, the one about the cabin doors now being secured. "You're stuck with me for a week."

Bailey lifts one well-shaped dark eyebrow and smiles wryly at me. "I think I can handle it."

"I don't know . . . rumor has it I'm a bit of a handful."

At this, Bailey chuckles, her full lips parting to reveal straight white teeth. Then she bites her lower lip and looks at me with a challenging expression. "Are you going to be a difficult patient?"

"Not planning on it." I shrug. "But if the mood

strikes me . . . I make no promises."

When the flight attendant swings by to offer us a cocktail and a ceramic dish of warm nuts, Bailey makes a pleased sound and pops a cashew into her mouth.

"Sorry," she says as she chews. "I've never been in first class before. This is freaking awesome."

"I'm glad you're enjoying it."

She looks at me like she's studying me while she chews. "This is probably all you're used to, isn't it?"

I nod, smirking. "Watching me fold myself into a seat back in coach would have probably been entertaining for you, but not so fun for me."

"I could see that." She nods, her gaze tracking down the length of me. "How tall are you these days?"

These days. Like it's changed recently. "Six-four."

She makes a low sound. "Sheesh. I'm five-one."

"Believe me, I noticed. Your sort of fun-sized."

I chuckle, and Bailey does the same, but not before elbowing me in the ribs.

Bailey's glass of champagne is delivered along with a sparkling water for me. Although I wasn't specifically instructed not to drink, I'm thinking head injuries and alcohol probably don't mix well, and it's safer to abstain for the time being.

The plane lurches forward and begins taxiing toward the runway. After a few minutes, we're cleared for takeoff and sailing smoothly en route to California. I fly every week for work, but I'm ashamed to admit that I haven't been home to visit my family in over two years.

"So, how are you feeling, really?" Bailey asks, sipping her champagne and eyeing me from her side of the large center console between us.

"A little dizziness that comes and goes. Some fatigue. Nothing major."

She hesitates, fiddling with her cocktail napkin before meeting my eyes again. "And with your, um, groin?"

I can't help but smirk. "Don't worry. I know it looked scary, but all systems still function perfectly."

"You know that's not what I meant."

"Fine. Well, it's sore as fuck, if you want to know the truth."

"I always want the truth," she says earnestly.

I study her then, really look at her, and my heart rate slowly begins to climb. "Thanks for doing this, Bailey," I say softly. Maybe going home for a week and relaxing on the beach is exactly what I need.

"You're welcome, Ashe."

I'm a big fan of the way my nickname sounds rolling off her gorgeous full lips. Apparently, so is my body, because my heart kicks into high gear, my blood thrumming steadily through my veins.

The flight gets underway, and since I've never spent any one-on-one time with Bailey, and I've certainly never flown with her before, so I have no idea if she wants to spend the flight talking or if she plans to read or watch a movie. But since she doesn't make a move to grab her phone or headphones, I don't either.

"So, who am I meeting?" she asks, rubbing her hands together like she's excited.

It's kind of freaking adorable. I figured she'd endure this week, at best. Being stuck with someone else's family for seven days seems like a very specific kind of torture.

"Everyone," I say. "My mom, sisters, my grandma, my aunt Darby . . . who makes the best peach pie on the planet. My inappropriate, crazy uncle Jim."

Bailey laughs, the sound soft and feminine. "Everyone has one of those, right?" she says teasingly.

"An inappropriate uncle? Totally. Standard issue. And I have three sisters, but you'll only meet the two younger ones. My oldest sister, Nora, would be there, but she's very pregnant right now. Didn't want to travel so close to the baby's due date."

"Aww, so you're going to be an uncle?"

"Yup. In a couple of weeks. It kind of feels like a technicality, though. There's a bunch of kids in the family, and they all feel like nieces and nephews rather than second cousins. Oh, which reminds me, my cousin Tad and his wife and family will be there, and so will my other cousins, Mack and Tyson."

"Any of them hot?" she asks.

I give her a pointed look, and she chuckles.

"Next question."

"Fine. Be a cock-block." She smirks. "Anything weird I should prepare myself for?"

"You mean other than my hot cousins trying to talk the panties off you?" I offer up a smile, but there's a weird knot of frustration stewing in my stomach.

Bailey doesn't seem to notice. She's too busy hunting through her dish of nuts to find the last cashew.

I hand her mine. "Here."

"Thanks."

"Actually, there is something, I guess. My parents are divorced, and they'll both be there, but my mom will be there with her new husband and my dad is still single. It's kind of our 'new norm'." I make air quotes with my fingers as I say this.

"Hmm. Okay." Bailey chews, looking thoughtful. "What else?"

I take a drink of my water, thinking about what other fun facts I can tell her about the Reed crew. "My grandma is called Lolli."

"Lolli?" One side of Bailey's mouth lifts with

a crooked smile.

"It used to be Lolli and Pop—my grandpa was Pop. He passed ten years ago, but her nickname had stuck by then."

"Lollipop. I think it's cute."

"She's a firecracker. You'll love her."

"I can't wait."

Strangely, neither can I.

We spend the entire flight talking, and then somehow, our plane is already touching down in San Diego as if no time has passed. Listening to Bailey's stories—about medical school, the odd jobs she's had over the years, and her cringe-worthy performance of Annie in high school—has kept me entertained, that's for sure.

As much as I resisted bringing a caretaker on this trip, I'm starting to realize that this week is going to be way more fun with Bailey by my side.

And that could be very, very dangerous.

CHAPTER FOUR

California Air

Bailey

Asher may have insisted on the plane that he has no plans of being a handful, but the second we touch down on the tarmac, he hits me with a piece of information that suggests the opposite.

He rented a car.

My first clue that this wasn't a regular rental car was that we didn't go to one of the rental car counters. Heck, we didn't even go to the rental car building at all. A guy dressed in a suit and dark sunglasses met us just outside the terminal and brought us the car.

And not just any car, mind you. A bright yellow convertible with a super-charged engine. I guess this is what happens when you're a celebrity or pro athlete—luxury car dealerships want you to be seen driving their brand. As we stand at the curb while our bags are loaded into the trunk, Asher doesn't seem to be giving any indication of giving up the keys.

"I just don't think that driving when your right leg is injured is a good idea, Ashe." I drop the handle of my rolling suitcase and fold my arms over my chest, making it quite clear that he's not winning this fight easily. "Maybe I should give Trey a call and clear this with him."

"He had no problem with me driving at home," Asher says, swinging the key ring around one thick finger as if he could hypnotize me into letting him have his way. "Besides, it's only a fifteen-minute drive. There's no way I'm passing up the opportunity to drive down the coast in this thing."

When Asher gives me a persuasive imitation of puppy-dog eyes and runs his fingers through his messy blond hair, suddenly I'm opening the door and sliding inside, resigned to riding shotgun. God, this man is lucky he's so damn good-looking. I have a feeling his looks have been getting him his way for a long time.

As I buckle my seat belt, it occurs to me that I'd better put a caveat on this whole *driving with a serious injury* situation. "If your leg gets tired or starts hurting again, you'd better pull this car over. Deal?"

He nods. "It's a deal." But the words are hardly out of his lips before he peels away from the terminal like a bat out of hell.

Holy speed demon. I grip the handle of the door, my knuckles instantly turning white.

"Jeez, Ashe!" I gasp. "You couldn't have rented something practical, like an SUV or something?"

He lets out a hearty, full-bodied laugh that puts a flutter in my stomach. "If we're going to do Southern California, we're doing it in style. And I figured you might need a proper getaway car when you realize how crazy my family is."

It's my turn to laugh. "I'm sure I can handle it."

A devilish grin twitches across Asher's lips as he flips down the sun visor and swerves into the far left lane, picking up speed. "You say that now. We'll see if you're singing that same tune after a few days with these weirdos."

The drive from the San Diego airport to where Asher's grandma lives on Coronado Island is absolutely stunning. I knew we would cross over water to get to the island, but when I get my first look at the Coronado Bridge, I flinch in my seat, pressing my hands over my eyes.

"I guess it's not a great time to tell you I'm scared of bridges," I say, peeking out at him from between my fingers.

"Not the best time, no," he says, his voice laced with concern. "I didn't know that about you."

I'm tempted to make a comment about how there are a lot of things he doesn't know about me. After all, in the two years we've known each other, we've only had a few one-on-one conversations, most of which were practically med-school pop quizzes. He'd ask me about some ache or pain he had, and I'd give him a medical explanation and tell him not to play so rough on the ice. Lather, rinse, repeat. I can't help but think that maybe if he'd listened to me, he wouldn't be facing the possibility of spending the rest of the season on the sidelines, but that's neither here nor there.

I pull in a slow, stuttering breath, trying to calm my ragged heartbeat.

"Would it help if I held your hand . . . for moral support?" He slides one big hand my way, palm up, but I swat it away.

"Yes. But in this instance I'm going to need both of your hands on the wheel. Ten and two, mister."

"Are you going to be all right?" he asks.

"I'll be okay. Just distract me until it's safe to look."

"Distract you. Can do. Have I told you the story about Lolli and the mechanical bull?"

Asher goes on to tell some story that I'm sure is riveting, but I don't soak any of it in. I'm too busy gazing down at the sparkling blue water as we cross over the San Diego Bay.

"You made it. We're on land again," Asher says, reassuring me.

"It's quite the view," I murmur, looking out into the distance now that my hands have left the comfort of my eyes.

The harbor is full of giant gray Navy ships sitting in water that's such a vibrant blue, it almost doesn't seem real. I take a deep breath, filling my lungs with the salty California air. It feels like the first real deep breath I've taken in years.

"This . . . this is gorgeous. Your grandmother lives here?"

Asher nods. "Pop used to work at the naval base down here, and when he got sick, Mom and Steve moved here to help take care of him. And then they all just stayed. I think we always thought Lolli would sell the place after Pop died, but she couldn't part with it. You'll see. It's a pretty amazing house."

And it turns out by *house*, he means *beachfront oasis*.

When we pull up to the quaint, two-story house, I'm immediately dazzled. The pale yellow house with pink shutters and an inviting front porch is absolutely adorable. There are two large palm trees in the front yard and a funky flamingo sculpture stuck into a flower bed.

"Welcome to Lolli's place," Asher says warmly as he shuts off the ignition and pops the trunk. "Are you ready to meet the fam?"

Ready or not, it doesn't matter. Because the next thing I know, we're not alone.

"Hey, everybody, Asher's here!" A petite old woman with a styled white pixie cut and sunglasses the size of dinner plates is standing on the porch, calling into the house. "Come on, you nincompoops! Don't make the old lady or the boy with the busted crotch carry all of his stuff!"

"That would be Lolli." Asher laughs, shaking his head in disbelief. "And if you hadn't guessed, I believe the boy with the busted crotch would be me."

"I pieced that together," I say with a giggle. "I'll get your bag. Go hug your grandma."

He gives me a stubborn look, but I'm not letting him win me over about this like he did in the driving argument. Besides, the least I can do is carry his bag so he can see the family who has probably missed the crap out of him.

When I make it to the porch, his duffel slung over one shoulder and my rolling suitcase in my other hand, a whole gaggle of relatives has joined Lolli on the porch, and each of them are fighting for their turn to hug Asher.

"You must be Dr. Bailey," Lolli says in a syrupy voice, and before I can stop her, she's pulling me tight into a hug with arms that are surprisingly strong for a woman of her age and stature.

"Lolli, let the poor girl go." A woman with graying blond hair unties the apron from her waist and swats Lolli with it, then introduces herself. "I'm Asher's mom. You can call me Tess." She shakes my hand, then gives the convertible a skeptical squint. "I'm guessing the sports car was my speed demon son's idea?"

My gaze flicks to Asher, a smirk twitching at the corner of my lips. "Yeah, Speedy Gonzalez insisted on driving despite his injury."

Asher holds up his hands in defense. "Hey now. I'm an excellent driver. Don't I at least get brownie points for distracting you so you didn't freak when we crossed the bridge?"

Tess pulls her son into a tight hug and kisses his scruffy jaw. "We're just giving you a hard time, honey. I couldn't be more thrilled that you're here."

"And I couldn't be more thrilled that we have an air-conditioned house!" Lolli fans her face to keep the sweat at bay. "Can we move this love fest inside before one of you has to mop me up off the porch?"

Asher grabs his duffel and slings it over his shoulder. "I'll lead the way."

Lead the way to what, you ask? A kitchen full of even more relatives to meet and greet. I'm going to need flash cards in order to remember everyone's name this week.

"Is there somewhere I can put our bags?" I ask Asher's mom, half yelling over the hubbub.

She nods, grabs Asher's duffel from off his shoulder, and motions for me to follow her upstairs, which I'm not so secretly relieved to do. *Holy family reunion*, there are a lot of people to meet at once. While they're all lovely so far, traveling always has the unique ability to make me sleepy, despite the fact that I've done nothing but sit in a plane and then a car.

I follow Tess down a long hall of rooms to a particularly sunny one at the end. It looks like this will be my home for the next week, and I must say, it's a whole lot nicer than the studio apartment I call home the rest of the year. There are beautiful framed pieces of abstract art on all the bright white walls, and the queen-sized bed in the center of the room is draped with a plush coral comforter and more throw pillows than I've ever seen outside of a home décor display.

"We figured you'd better have the room nearest to Asher's in case there's some medical emergency at night," Tess says, lingering in the doorway as I leave my suitcase next to the dresser. "I'm no doctor, but if you need any help with him, I can give you my number. Steve and I live just down the street."

"Maybe you're not a medical professional, but you *are* his mother. I'm sure you nursed many a hockey injury of Asher's when he was a kid."

She laughs, her eyes kind when they meet mine. "I took care of plenty of injuries that probably should have been the responsibility of an emergency room. It's a relief to pass on the torch to an actual professional."

We've been absent from the family gathering for all of five minutes, but apparently, that's a few minutes too long. A voice that is unmistakably Lolli's comes thundering from the kitchen and up to the rafters, telling us to "get your tushes back down here."

A giggle escapes me. Asher wasn't kidding. His grandmother is a firecracker.

Back in the kitchen, the hugging has stopped, but the chaos is far from over.

While one of Asher's relatives takes notes of everyone's preferred pizza toppings for dinner tonight, another is helping Lolli press snickerdoodle dough onto pans. And in the center of all of this, Asher is sitting at the breakfast bar, halfway through telling his aunt and uncle the story of how his injury happened. Or at least *his* version, which sounds more like a horror story. I'm sensing some exaggeration going on, so I interrupt him halfway through a description that makes the player who body-checked him sound like a rabid Sasquatch on skates.

"I hate to interrupt the sports talk, guys, but I need to get my patient here set up with an ice pack. It's been a long morning already."

Lolli, who's had her pointer fingers stuffed in her ears to keep from hearing the gory details of Asher's injury, leaps at the chance to volunteer a bag of frozen peas from her freezer, which I happily accept. Trey sent along a bunch of instant cold packs, but they're all still packed somewhere in my luggage.

"Mind if I head to the screened-in porch?" Asher tilts his head toward the sliding glass door at the back of the kitchen. "Might as well feel a little sunshine on my skin while I ice this thing."

Frozen peas in hand, I follow him through the sliding glass door, which he pulls closed behind me before situating himself on a wicker chair facing the beach. A soft drizzle has started to fall, although the sun is still shining full force. With the smell of rain mixing perfectly with the sweet, sugary smell of the snickerdoodle bars Lolli has in the oven, I feel like I'm breathing in a deep breath of pure happiness.

"So, was I right or was I right?" Asher asks, lifting his leg onto the matching wicker ottoman in front of him.

I crouch down level with Asher's leg so I can check the swelling on his thigh. Surprisingly, it's not as bad as I thought it would be after a full morning of travel.

"Right about what?" I ask, hitching up his shorts to the pale skin of his inner thigh.

Asher doesn't blink, even though my hands are damn close to his underwear. "My family. They're crazy."

I shake my head, positioning the bag of peas against the most swollen part of his inner thigh. "They aren't crazy. They're sweet. There's just so many of them. It's a lot to take in at once."

Asher flinches a little at the cold of our make-shift ice pack. I have to admit; it's kind of cute. He may be a big tough hockey player, but he's still a little sensitive to a bag of frozen peas.

"Well, I know it can be overwhelming," he

says, "but it means the world to me that you offered to come here with me. If it wasn't for you, I wouldn't have come. I didn't want some random team doctor here watching my every move and scrutinizing everything I did. I haven't seen some of these people in years, so . . . thank you."

I can hardly believe it, but for the first time, I'm seeing Asher's guard come down a little. I've never seen this tender side of him before. It's intriguing. As a cloud shifts in the sky, the sunlight hits his blue eyes just right. They're nearly the color of the ocean, and just as mesmerizing.

"So, maybe your injury was a blessing in disguise." I lay a reassuring hand on his shoulder with a gentle squeeze. "An excuse to have some time off to visit your family."

Asher scoffs, and I drop my hand. "Yeah. Something like that."

He's not convinced, and who could blame him? I wouldn't be looking for silver linings either if an injury were keeping me from doing what I love more than anything in the world.

"Hey." I tug at the sleeve of his T-shirt, and he swings his gaze back to me, those sapphire eyes locking with mine again. "We can't control everything. I know it sucks, but maybe it was fate."

His frown softens into a skeptical smile. "Fate? Do you believe in that? I thought you'd be too scientific for that kind of thing."

A smile lingers on my lips as I push up to my feet. "Maybe I'm losing my touch, being on my first break from med school in four years."

"I think it's just the California air getting to you," he says, adjusting the bag of peas. "Be careful. All that sunshine and salt water will make you do some crazy things."

My cheeks start to warm, and I don't think it's from the sun beating in through the huge picture windows. California air or no California air, with the way Asher is squinting those sultry blue eyes at me, I'm not so worried about *saying* something crazy as *doing* something crazy.

There's just one little thing stopping me. And by one little thing, I mean eight little things . . . in the form of Asher's family members who are probably watching us through the sliding glass door right now.

Heaven help me. This is going to be a long week.

CHAPTER FIVE

Unicorns, Dad Jokes, and Inappropriate Public
Erections

Asher

Balancing a plate of pizza on my knees, I grab a
napkin from my aunt Darby as she passes by
in a flourish. Dinnertime is a casual affair tonight,
and complete chaos, of course. Kids are running
through the house playing tag, pizza boxes litter
the kitchen island, and the TV is set on a volume
only Lolli would appreciate.

"I don't know. Go ask your uncle Asher," I hear
my cousin Tad say in the other room. It's a common phrase when I'm in the house.

If I didn't have such a massive headache right
now, I'd be happy to entertain the kids. But the
truth is I'm not feeling so hot, and I'm craving
peace and quiet. Something I have no chance of

getting tonight, by the looks of things.

But mere seconds later, my cousin's daughter Fable bounds into the room, and all three-and-a-half feet of her is practically vibrating with excitement.

She stops before me with an inquisitive look painted on her delicate features. "Uncle Asher, is the road just a really big sidewalk for cars?"

I shift in my seat, shoving one hand through my hair as I consider her question. "Uh, I guess so."

She nods, seeming pleased with herself. "I think there was a unicorn in my room last night. I saw sprinkles."

"That sounds . . . fascinating." I smile at her, and from the corner of my eye, I can see Bailey watching us from across the room. Her mouth is soft and relaxed, and there's a warm look in her eyes as she watches me interact with the precocious six-year-old.

"I think my mom was abducted by aliens," Fable says next, capturing my attention again.

"Why do you think that?" I ask, studying her with a serious expression.

Her blond hair is a wild mess of waves and

tangles, and her eyes are bright and curious. "Because. Normally she smells like cheese, and today she smelled like plastic." Her eyes widen dramatically as they latch onto mine. "It's weird, don't you think?"

"Hmm . . ." Before I can even contemplate more of a response than that, she twirls around, spinning quickly, and stops dramatically with her hands on her hips.

"Do you know how I did that? Magic," she announces proudly. "I'm magical!"

I nod, giving her a big smile. "You are, and you're also very clever. What other moves have you got?"

Fable thinks it over as her younger sister, Brooke, toddles over to where I'm sitting. She's two and is as cute as a button, but when she gets close, a terrible smell descends upon us.

"Hey, princess," I say, patting her head.

She shoves one sticky finger in her mouth, watching me with huge bright blue eyes.

"Hey, Tad," I call toward the other room. "I think the little one needs a diaper change."

I hear a muttered phrase I can't make out, which

may very well be one of the made-up curse words Tad's created to say around the girls, and then he appears, rounding the corner.

"Fable's got some interesting theories," I say to him as he scoops up Brooke in his arms.

His nose scrunches as he gets a whiff of what she's been cooking up. "Yeah. She keeps us on our toes." Then he lifts Brooke up in the air and grins at her. "Just give this one a few years to master her bowels, and then she'll be taking over the world too."

I chuckle and look down to meet Fable's eyes. "Okay, smart girl. As much as I love listening to your amazing stories, I'm going to spend some time with my friend Bailey, okay?"

Fable nods once and then dashes away. "I'll save ya a snickerdoodle!" she calls over one slim shoulder without slowing down. She really is a sweet kid.

Bailey grins as I approach, folding her napkin. "You're good with them."

I nod. "They're fun—for the most part. But I draw the line at diaper changes."

She scoffs, pushing a half-eaten slice of pizza

across her plate. "Don't tell me you're going to be one of *those* dads."

I quickly shake my head. "My own kids? No problem. Dirty diapers don't scare me. But, hey, I didn't exactly hear you volunteering to change her."

Bailey laughs, shaking her head. "Fair enough."

"How are you holding up?" I ask, meeting her eyes.

Her mouth presses into a line. "I'm fine. I'm more worried about you. All this noise and chatter can't be easy on you, and I've seen you rub your temples a couple of times."

I give my head a small shake, feeling warmth spread through my chest at the thought of her paying such close attention to how I've been feeling. "I've been better. You okay with eating outside?"

She nods. "But I don't think it's any quieter out on the deck."

She's right, of course. The two outside tables are filled with my relatives, eating slices of pizza off paper plates, telling stories and laughing.

"Let's take our plates and go down to the beach," I suggest instead.

Bailey leads the way through the house and out the screen door. I grab a beach towel from the basket on the back deck and then follow her down the stairs and onto the sand that feels cool beneath my bare feet. The sun is sinking slowly on the horizon, a lazy orange blob hovering in the distance over the water. Balancing my plate with one hand, I spread out the towel with the other.

"Oh, this is a good idea," she says, watching me closely before reaching out and taking my plate from me so I don't drop it on the sand.

I straighten out the towel and grab my plate back from her. "Take a seat."

"Thanks." She lowers herself to the colorful towel, folding her legs beneath her.

I join her and take a bite of my pizza. The sound of the waves crashing in the distance drowns out the cacophony of my family's voices. *Ah. Much better.*

But our silent reprieve doesn't last long because two familiar voices approach from the direction of the house.

I turn, and when I spot my sisters, Courtney and Amber, heading our way, I rise to my feet. They squeal when they see me, jogging the last few steps.

"Hey, stranger!" Amber says, throwing her arms around my waist in a hug. Only seventeen months apart, we've always been close, but it's been a while since I've seen her. She's a high-profile marketing executive and lives in New York City where her career is her life.

"Did you guys just get in?" I ask, pulling Courtney in for a hug next.

"Yup," they confirm in unison.

My youngest sister Courtney is a special education teacher. Since she gets the summers off, she's usually able to come visit me in Seattle and stay for a week every summer.

The moment their attention swings to Bailey, who has now risen to her feet too, a wide smile takes over Courtney's face, and Amber looks downright shocked.

I knew my mom told them that I'd be bringing a nurse with me at the team's insistence. But Bailey, in her cut-off denim shorts and purple halter top that barely conceals her curves, doesn't look like any nurse I've ever seen. The open bottle of beer suspended in midair halfway to her lips might have something to do with it too.

"This is my friend Bailey," I say, gesturing toward her. "She's my medical chaperone this week."

Amber offers her a polite smile, and Courtney pulls her in for a hug.

"It's so nice to meet you," Courtney says excitedly.

Bailey's face lights up with a smile as she returns my youngest sister's hug. "You must be Ashe's sisters."

"Yup," Courtney says, and introduces herself. "I'm the baby of the family at twenty-four."

"And I'm Amber. Second oldest of the bunch." She opts to leave out her age, something I've found that people over twenty-nine tend to do. "So, you're a nurse?"

"A doctor, actually. But I'm really here as Asher's friend. The team is just being overly cautious."

"So you're okay?" Courtney asks me, her blue eyes meeting mine with a hint of worry.

"I will be. Trust me, I've dealt with much worse."

The hardest part of my injury, in all honesty, is feeling that I've let my team down. They have a game tomorrow, and I'm not sure I can bring myself to watch it without punching something or throwing up from nerves. I hate that I won't be out on the ice to help them. In a playoff game, no less.

Of course, even if I were still in Seattle, it's not like Coach would have allowed me at the arena to cheer them on from the bench. Apparently, a loud and noisy stadium with its bright flashing lights isn't the best place to recover from a concussion. So instead, here I am, on a beach for some rest and relaxation—at least, that's what it's supposed to be. Coach doesn't need to know that, on occasion, my family is even louder and more enthusiastic than a stadium full of rowdy hockey fans.

The four of us settle onto the sand, and I listen as my sisters—well, mostly Courtney—fire off questions at Bailey, which she fields like a pro.

"What's your specialty?" Courtney asks.

Bailey smiles. "Internal medicine."

"So, you didn't actually study sports medicine?" Amber's eyes narrow the slightest bit.

Retract the claws, Amber. I'm fine. Thankfully, I resist the urge to roll my eyes and maintain my composure. I'm sure Bailey can handle herself around my sisters, no matter how much I want to jump in and come to her rescue.

"No, I didn't." Bailey glances at me. "But your brother's injuries are conditions I'm familiar with. I know all the warning signs to look for, and the complications that can arise. I promise, he's in good hands."

Courtney smiles happily at her, and even Amber seems somewhat mollified, leaning back on the sand.

When my baby sister's line of questioning moves to whether Bailey is single, I decide it's time to call it a night, and I push to my feet. "I think I'm ready to turn in. We had a long day of travel."

Bailey stands and dusts the sand from the back of her denim shorts. "It was nice meeting both of you. See you in the morning?"

"We'll be here," Courtney says enthusiastically.

Once inside, Bailey thanks Lolli for welcoming her here, and then starts up the stairs.

I grab a bottle of water for myself and another for Bailey, and then say good night to a few of my relatives in the kitchen. Lolli kisses my cheek and shoves two snickerdoodle bars wrapped in paper towels into my hand.

"Bailey is lovely," Lolli whispers with a wink when I pull back. "She'll make some lucky guy very happy someday."

"Uh . . ." I stammer, instantly feeling my pulse thrumming in my throat. "Yeah, she's cool."

Lolli's mouth curves into a smile as she watches me for a second longer while lifting one brow.

NOTE TO SELF: Do not bring a single female friend to a family function ever again, because apparently my relatives have zero chill when it comes to picturing me in a relationship. It doesn't exactly help my cause that Bailey is stunning and has a personality to match. She possesses a smile that can render anyone speechless, and she just happens to be a freaking doctor.

"'Night, Mom," I call into the living room where she's sitting with Steve and my aunt Darby, gossiping about something.

"'Night, honey. I'm so glad you're here. Make sure you tell Bailey thanks for me."

"Will do," I call back.

Climbing the stairs isn't the easiest thing I've ever done. In a graceless uneven hobble, I eventually make it to the top. I head to the end of the hall and consider knocking on Bailey's door, which has been left open a crack.

With a deep breath, I decide against it. I really do need a shower. Maybe I'll see if she's still up when I'm done.

When I finish in the shower, I dress quickly in a clean pair of cotton shorts and a white T-shirt, and then grab the dessert and water bottles I snagged from the kitchen earlier, before padding barefoot across the hall.

After tapping on Bailey's door, I take a step back and wait.

"Come in," she calls.

When I enter, her back is turned, and she's wrestling with the zipper on her suitcase in the corner. My gaze drops to her curvy ass in those denim shorts, and my body reacts to the view, my chest tightening and everything south of my waistband growing heavy.

Bailey turns and pushes a strand of hair from her face. "Hey."

"Let me." I place our dessert on the dresser and get to work on freeing the stuck zipper.

"Thanks."

Once the suitcase is open, I place it on her bed. "No problem. I brought you something." I tip my head toward the dresser.

"Yum. Thank you. And I should probably ice you before you go to bed too."

I shift my weight and then sit down on the edge of her bed. "I can do it myself."

She nods. "Whatever you want. Just want to make sure I'm earning my keep."

And I want to make sure I don't have a repeat of this afternoon's episode, where I almost got a hard-on while she was busy wedging a bag of frozen peas under the edge of my boxer briefs. It wasn't my finest moment. Thankfully, the chill success-fully zapped any misplaced lust I was feeling. Bailey's here this week to tend to my injuries, not my sorely neglected dick.

"Oh, you showered." Her gaze roams up to my towel-dried hair. "That sounds heavenly right now."

"I don't know what it is about traveling that makes you feel so disgusting."

With a nod of agreement, Bailey crosses over

to her suitcase and begins removing bright articles of clothing—a pink bikini, stacks of T-shirts, and shorts—and places them inside the empty dresser drawers. She sets a tank top and a pair of silky pajama shorts on top of the dresser, making a happy noise as she works.

There's something I like about watching her make herself at home here. Like she's breathing life into this room that normally sits empty.

She quickly grabs a handful of underthings—lacy bras and satin panties—and shoves them into the top drawer before sliding it shut. It's then I realize that maybe I'm intruding. Maybe she doesn't want me in here, lounging across her bed while she unpacks her underwear.

We've traveled together before, and one time in particular comes to mind, last summer when our entire group of friends camped in the San Juan islands. The vivid mental image of her excitedly jumping up and down and grabbing my bicep when we spotted an orca in the bay comes to mind. This is definitely different from camping with a dozen other people, though.

"Maybe I should go," I say, clearing my throat.

She shakes her head. "Let's have our dessert

first. Then I can shower."

Bailey retrieves the water bottles from the dresser and tosses me one. It lands on the bed beside me with a soft bounce. Then she brings both snickerdoodle bars over, and after unwrapping the paper towels, sort of measures the bars against each other.

Fuck, she's adorable.

"Here. You can take the bigger one. You're practically twice my size."

I chuckle. "I already had three downstairs. Take whichever one you want."

Bailey smiles, then helps herself to the larger of the two, which in turn makes me smile. Then we both take a bite as she settles on the bed beside me.

"Oh, these are going to be dangerous." She moans, closing her eyes.

I lick my lips as I watch her chew, the delicate column of her throat working as she swallows her first bite. I'll bet her mouth would taste like cinnamon and sugar if I kissed her right now.

Why the hell am I thinking about kissing her? Way to cross the line, dickhead.

It's day one, and my thoughts are already in the gutter. Owen's stern warning about behaving myself around Bailey replays in my head, and his fears suddenly don't seem so far-fetched.

With another small noise of pleasure, Bailey licks a crystal of sugar from her lower lip. I shove the rest of my dessert into my mouth, chew, and swallow it without tasting a thing. I could've just eaten a piece of a roof shingle and I wouldn't have known the difference.

Dragging my gaze away from her mouth, I focus on the abstract painting hanging on the wall across from the bed, bold yellow slashes of paint on a white canvas. I hope Lolli didn't pay much for that thing. I could recreate it in about three minutes.

Still needing to get my head out of the gutter, I decide to bring up my mother. "My mom said to tell you thanks for being here."

Bailey finishes her dessert and takes a sip of water. "That's very sweet of her. Your mom seems really great. Steve too."

I shrug. "I've heard Steve say about six words in as many years, but yeah, he's nice. He makes my mom happy, and that's what matters."

We're quiet for a moment, and I shift so I'm

facing her. "You have everything you need?"

Bailey nods, her wide eyes watching me as I lounge casually beside her.

There's a moment of hesitation, a moment where I know I should get up from her bed and leave, but I don't. Or rather I can't, because Bailey is leaning back on her elbows like I am, mirroring me, and only a foot of space separates her lips from mine. Her gaze drops to my mouth, and my heart rate triples.

My brain is screaming at me, *Abort! Abort!* So before I do something stupid—like kiss her—I hop to my feet quicker than I should. Wincing at the flash of pain in my groin, I half walk, half limp toward the door.

Bailey gets to her feet and joins me in the doorway. "Sore?" she asks, concern in her voice and in her kind eyes that stare back at me.

Nodding, I lean one hip against the door frame. "I think I'm just tired."

"You don't have to be a tough guy around me," she says softly, placing one hand on my chest. "You have to tell me when you hurt so I can help you."

"I know," I say, my voice deep, husky.

"Let me tape it up for you tomorrow."

I nod. "Okay."

Bailey gives me a look, a mothering type of expression that says *you're in a lot of trouble*. Definitely not one that screams *I want you to kiss the hell out of me*.

Noted.

"Make sure you ice it." Her voice is stern. "At least twenty minutes."

"I will. Good night." With a deep breath, I shuffle across the hall to my room and fall back onto the bed.

When I break a cold pack in half and shake it to activate the dry ice, my dick is more than half hard. And even when I shove the ice pack into my underwear, it doesn't let up.

Awesome.

Real fucking awesome.

Being here with Bailey in such close quarters is messing with my head, more than I thought possible. Watching her interact with Lolli. Defending herself to Amber, and promising that I'm in good hands. Looking after me. Fuck, offering me the bigger of the two desserts.

I don't know what's happening to me, but it's obvious something is.

Even though my body's enthusiastic response has yet to fade, I'm too tired to jerk off, which is saying something, because it's normally a nightly occurrence. Maybe this concussion is messing with my head more than I thought.

Sighing, I grab the pill bottle from beside my bed and shake a couple of painkillers into my mouth, then swallow them without water, grimacing at the bitter taste left in my mouth.

Then I close my eyes and drift off into a restless sleep, wondering what Bailey would have done if I'd leaned over and kissed her.

CHAPTER SIX

Geronimo

Bailey

After four years of nonstop work and study, I almost forgot what it's like to just relax. But today, I'm getting plenty of practice.

Despite my best efforts to help out around the house, everyone has been insistent that taking care of Asher should be my only concern and focus this week. When I volunteered to help Lolli and Tess prep sloppy joes for lunch, they shooed me out of the kitchen, insisting that I should go check on Asher's leg again, or see how his head is feeling. It's like they don't want me to leave his side.

And for the most part, I haven't. Asher and I have passed the morning and the better part of the afternoon lounging in the backyard, only getting out of our lawn chairs to move them when we're no longer in the shade. We've done so much sitting around today, that my chair will probably have a divot in the shape of my backside when I finally get up.

"Do we get to do this all week?" I push my sunglasses down my nose to look Asher in the eye, but he's busy applying a thin coat of sunblock. I get momentarily distracted, watching his bulky muscles flex as he rubs the cream over his sculpted shoulders.

"Ty will probably insist on us going surfing at least once. And the girls usually go shopping at some point. But, otherwise, you're looking at the extent of a Reed family reunion." He stretches his arms wide, gesturing to the beauty that is our current situation.

"I don't know about surfing." I give him a pointed look.

He waves me off. "Trust me, it'll be little more than me paddling around on a board looking like an idiot while my cousins tease me for being lame."

I nod, and then look around, enjoying the feel of the sunshine on my skin.

The pool is packed with little ones, the sky doesn't have a single cloud, and we've got zero obligations. *Perfect.*

I'm not sure if I expected his family to treat him any differently because he's a pro player in an elite sport, or because his talents earned him a multi-million-dollar contract, but that's the last thing they do. To everyone, Asher is just a member of the family. A brother, a son, a grandson. My heart warms at that realization.

He's still expected to clear his plate from the table and take out the garbage when it's full. There's no one pulling him aside to ask for money, and no one requests an autograph on a T-shirt for their friend's coworker's son. I'm pleasantly surprised by this. To be made a celebrity in your own family would certainly be exhausting. Asher came here for some downtime and to heal, and I'm happy to see that is exactly what he's getting.

To that end, they also don't seem overly concerned with his injuries. His mother asked me about them in the bedroom when we first arrived, but it was with the nonchalance of someone inquiring if the peaches were ripe at the farmers' market. I'm guessing it's because she's seen her son injured many times over the years, and worse than this at some point. It's kind of refreshing being here—where everyone behaves like adults, and there's no gossiping or judgment. I can't say the same would be true in my own family.

I could spend the entire week planted in this chair and not regret a single moment of it.

Oh, relaxation. How I have missed you.

"Mind if we join you?" a voice asks over my shoulder.

I turn to find Asher's sisters pulling up lawn chairs. "The more, the merrier, Courtney and Amber." I've been making a point to use people's names as much as possible to commit them to memory.

Thank you, med school, for making me a pro at memorizing things quickly.

I've been silently quizzing myself all day, saying people's names in my head every time they walk past me to take a dip in the pool or run inside for a snack. Tyson is the one with the scruff, whereas Mack is clean shaven. *S* for silent is also *S* for Steve, Tess's incredibly quiet hubby.

I wrap up yet another round of the "Name That Person" exam as Courtney and Amber set up their chairs, but when I look over to the steps of the porch, an unfamiliar face is heading our way. This must be my extra-credit question. Whoever she is, she's wearing a sunny yellow dress that hugs the roundness of her baby bump, the size of which, by my estimate, should put her well into her third trimester.

Not that I'll be the first to bring that up.

I live by the rule of never mentioning a woman's pregnancy until she or someone else brings it up first. It's the best way to avoid accidentally asking someone when her due date is, just to find out she's bloated from eating one too many snickerdoodle bars. Trust me, I've heard the horror stories.

When Asher spots our new guest, his face lights up and he springs out of his chair, running toward her with the enthusiasm of a golden retriever chasing after a ball. I have to admit, it's pretty freaking adorable.

"Holy sh—shiitake mushrooms." He barely catches himself, mindful of the audience of young ears nearby as he pulls our newest guest into a massive hug. "I didn't think you were coming, Nora!"

I mentally place the name. Nora. This must be Asher's oldest—and very pregnant, due any day—sister.

"Watch the bump, watch the bump!" She wiggles her way out of the hug, one hand protectively on her round belly. "The more you squish the little devil, the more he or she kicks like a soccer player with something to prove, and he or she is running out of real estate in there as it is."

Bingo. That's a green light on the baby talk.

"And that's exactly why I didn't think you'd be here," Asher says, giving her baby bump a gentle apology tap. "It can't be easy to travel when you look like a balloon about to pop."

Nora rolls her eyes. "Gee, thanks. That makes me feel great about how I look."

"You know what I mean."

"And *you* know that I wouldn't miss a chance to see you for anything in the world, ready to pop or not. So, here I am. Todd is inside unpacking, if you want to go say hi."

Asher's smile creeps up to his eyes. "Heck yeah. I need to throw my swimsuit on anyway. Do you want anything while I'm inside, Nor?"

"What I *want* is a beer," she says with a laugh. "But what I need is something to eat. Could you grab me whatever leftovers are in the fridge? The snack I ate on the drive isn't cutting it."

As Asher bounds up the wooden steps and into the house, Amber hops out of her lawn chair so her pregnant sister can sit.

"So, how are you feeling, Nor?" she asks.

Nora responds with an enormous yawn. "Tired, obviously. And hot. Being pregnant in the summer is tough."

"But how is it being pregnant? Is it magical? Tell us the truth," Courtney says with a wistful sigh and stars in her eyes. I can tell she's the romantic of the group.

Nora heaves out a long sigh. I have little doubt that she's about to drop a truth bomb on us, and I kind of already love her. "I can't get comfortable enough to sleep for longer than ten minutes at a time. I have terrible heartburn. I always have to pee. All. The. Time."

"Hang in there, sis. It'll all be worth it," Amber says, the more practical of the two.

Nora rolls her eyes dramatically. "That's what they keep telling me."

I decide against adding my own commentary. I highly doubt Nora would appreciate knowing about hemorrhoids or preeclampsia or any of the other horrible things that can happen to pregnant women.

"Anyone know how to make this kid come sooner?" Nora asks after a moment of silence.

"Ask Bailey," Courtney says. "She's a *doctor.*" She wiggles her eyebrows in a way that I know I'll read into later.

Nora looks confused for a moment before a flicker of recognition sparks in her eyes. "Right, you must be the medical supervision the team required for Asher. Mom mentioned that." The lawn chair squeaks as she leans forward to shake my hand. "Good to meet you, Dr. Bailey."

"I'm not quite Dr. Bailey yet," I admit. "I still have my residency left before I'm done with medical school."

"She's going to be an intern," Courtney says.

"An *internist*," Amber says, correcting her.

"Whatever. Same difference."

A collective laugh bubbles out of all of us, and for a second, I feel like I know what it's like to have sisters.

"So, what's your story, Bailey?" Nora asks.

"I just accepted a position in Seattle, but it doesn't start for a couple of weeks. I've been friends with your brother for a while now, and so when he needed the help, I wasn't about to pass up a free trip to the beach."

She nods. "That's cool. I know my mom and Lolli are over the moon that Asher was able to come."

"It's been a blast so far. I'm an only child, so being around a big family is a treat." I watch another kiddo jump into the pool.

"Hopefully you're able to relax a little too. I can't imagine your schedule allows for a lot of that," Nora says.

"Hear, hear." I lift my bottle of water in a toast.

Grinning, I look out at the kids splashing in the pool. Fable, the spunky little blonde who was running all of her best theories past Asher yesterday, has appointed herself the only judge of a cannonball contest. She's sitting poolside with her tiny toes in the water, shouting out scores as the other kids take turns jumping off the diving board. Dressed in denim shorts and a slouchy white V-neck, I've been careful to stay out of their splash zone.

"There's always room for one more in the family, you know," Courtney says, abandoning all attempts at subtlety. "So, have you and Asher been strictly friends all this time?"

"Did I just hear my name?"

Asher reappears with a pile of potato chips and a sloppy joe on a paper plate, which he passes off to Nora. His mom and cousins are following close behind him, but I hardly notice. I'm a little too focused on the shirtless Greek god of a man standing in front of me, his black swim trunks hanging temptingly low on his trim waist.

It's said that humans only use a tiny portion of their brains. If that's true, 99 percent of mine is focused on Asher's deliciously sinful body. Six-pack abs. Broad shoulders. Trim waist. Perfectly disheveled hair. A playful smile that suggests he's always down for some mischief.

God, why does he have to be so freaking attractive? And why did I elect to come on this trip when I'm so sex-deprived? For a smart chick, I can be pretty freaking stupid sometimes.

It's not like I haven't seen Asher shirtless before. Last summer, when our friend group went camping off the coast, I think we spent at least half the trip in swimsuits. Not to mention our awkward moment at the Ice Hawks' charity calendar shoot. Even though I have nothing but fond memories of that day. Rubbing oil on his sculpted chest wasn't exactly a hardship.

Looking at him now, where I'm close enough to count each muscle in his six-pack, I can honestly say he looks more rugged and muscular than any male model I've seen in a magazine ad. And those pictures are photoshopped. Asher is the real deal.

"Well, if you're going to talk about me while I'm gone, you'd better at least tell me what you were saying." He reaches to snag a chip off of Nora's plate, but she slaps his wrist away.

"We were just telling Bailey about your famous cannonball," Amber says, obviously improvising. "How you used to be able to splash Mom through the kitchen window if she left it open. Remember that?"

"*I* certainly remember," Tess says, rolling her eyes at her son.

He responds with a cocky grin and pretends to brush the dust off his shoulders. "Not my fault I have the best cannonball in the game."

Seconds later, Fable, who must have the hearing of a bat to have picked up on our conversation, is scampering over to us, leaving tiny wet footprints along the concrete behind her.

"Uncle Asher, Uncle Asher! You gotta be in the cannonball contest!"

She's flailing her arms in excitement, but Asher doesn't meet her level of enthusiasm. In fact, his cocky stance melts into a more sheepish one as he rakes his fingers through his hair, looking apologetically down at little Fable.

"Not this year, princess."

She stamps one foot. "Why not?"

"Because I don't want to. Plus, I bet Dr. Bailey wouldn't want me to do that with my bad leg, right, Bailey?"

When he glances my way with pleading eyes, looking for backup, I just shrug. "One jump in the pool isn't going to make or break your recovery."

"Seeee? Please, Uncle Asher?" Fable pushes out her lower lip and bats her big blue eyes. "Just one time? For me?"

Asher gives me a *thanks for nothing* look.

Nice try. I'm on Fable's side with this one.

"What? Are you all talk and no walk?" I say,

taunting him. "I thought you said you had the best cannonball in the game."

Not one to back down from a challenge, he removes his watch and places it on the table, then looks at me with a devilish glint in his eyes. "Do you have your phone on you?"

I pat my empty pockets. "It's in my room. Why?"

He doesn't answer. He just prowls toward me.

When it finally dawns on me what's about to happen, Asher's hands are already gripping my waist, scooping me up out of my lawn chair and tossing me over his shoulder, fireman style.

"No-no-no-no-no!" I half laugh, half squeal, kicking my feet in protest.

But it's too late. We're already barreling toward the pool, and a second later, he yells out "GERONIMO!" and makes the plunge.

Everything is a blur of blue—first the sky, then the water as we break through the surface, creating a splash big enough to make a tidal wave feel insufficient. And when we emerge, laughing and gasping for air, I'm instantly swimming in the cobalt of Asher's eyes. He shoots me the proudest smile, not for a second loosening the grip he has on my hips.

"Gotcha."

His voice is so husky and sweet, it sends a tremor right through me. Maybe it's just the shock of the cold water to my system, but all my nerves are suddenly hyperalert to every flex and shift of his muscles beneath my fingertips.

For a perfect moment, it's just him and me, bobbing with the give and take of the water, laughing and holding each other tightly with no intention of letting go. His gaze moves to my mouth, and my heart pounds hard and fast. There's an instinct, a stirring in the pit of my stomach, telling me I should lean in and kiss that cocky grin right off his mouth.

But then the universe reminds me why I can't.

A sweet, squeaky little voice calls out our score, a made-up number somewhere in the zillion-billion-trillion range, and pulls me back into reality. And here in reality, cannonball contests are a spectator sport, and Asher's entire family is watching as his volunteer nurse has her hands all over his half-naked body.

"I, um, need to dry off." I reluctantly let go of the world's hottest flotation device and kick furiously toward the ladder. There are too many eyes on us, and I need to remove myself from this situation before everyone sees me blush.

Thankfully, Tess passes me a towel the instant I'm out of the pool, which I wrap around my torso. I'm not trying to be the sole participant in a wet T-shirt contest, and no one needs any more reasons to stare right now.

Dodging the looks from Asher's family, I excuse myself and head inside to go change into something dry. Once I've wrangled my wet hair into a messy bun and swapped my wet clothes for dry ones, I head down to the kitchen to find a glass of water. What I find instead is Lolli, mixing a pitcher of some yellowish concoction with a long wooden spoon.

"Quite the splash you made there." She gives me a knowing smile over her shoulder as she pulls two glasses down from the cabinet, filling both to the brim with whatever she's been mixing. "You look like you could use a drink of Lolli's special juice."

She nudges one glass toward me. Although I usually prefer beer to mixed drinks, I raise it to my lips.

Holy cow, a little goes a long way with this stuff. This has to be one part pineapple juice to three parts vodka, with Lord knows what else thrown in. I must not have much of a poker face, because Lolli gets a kick out of my reaction to her cocktail.

"Yeah, it'll put some hair on your chest. Or whatever the girl equivalent of that is. Take it one sip at a time."

While we watch the sunset begin outside the kitchen window, Lolli and I make small talk, covering a variety of topics.

I can't even concentrate on the words coming out of my mouth. Because although I may have ditched my wet clothes, I can't ditch the feeling that whatever just happened between Asher and me was more than just a little poolside prank.

It shouldn't have meant anything. I gave him a hard time about not wanting to do his cannonball, so he retaliated by dragging me in with him. Simple as that.

So, why am I still reeling?

I knew coming into this trip that I'd be dealing with a smoking-hot patient. What I didn't know was that putting my hands on his muscular chest would leave my fingertips buzzing well over an hour later. There's no doubt that the sexual chemistry between us is very real, and I'm starting to think it's not just coming from my side. Thinking about the hungry way he looked at my mouth makes my toes curl even now.

That, or I just really, really need to get laid. It's been too dang long.

As the sun sinks lower and lower in the sky, I'm surprised to find the amount of Lolli's special juice in my glass getting lower too. When Lolli notices, she refills it without a second thought. I think grandmothers are allergic to empty glasses and empty plates. Even when Tad and Steve wander inside to grab hot dogs and buns, announcing they're firing up the grill, Lolli and I keep at it—enjoying girl talk and some quiet time inside.

"And then I told him, 'Listen, buddy, I've got a full life here. I don't need an elderly Prince Charming to save me,'" Lolli says with a laugh, and I realize that I haven't been paying nearly close enough attention to her stories.

Gradually, the other family members start to filter inside too. Mosquitoes are starting to bite, and the little ones are up past their bedtimes. Come to think of it, as I approach the bottom of my second glass of whatever the heck Lolli is serving me,

I may need to go to bed soon too.

But when Asher walks through that sliding glass door, his tan line peeking out from above the elastic of his swim trunks, I have a little bit of a different idea about what bedtime might mean for me tonight. Maybe we can take the chemistry I've been feeling for a spin.

Draining the last of my drink, I stand up on slightly wobbly legs, trying to mask the fact that I'm definitely feeling the alcohol in my system. Asher has already headed upstairs, so I quickly thank Lolli for the drinks, say a general good-night to anyone else hanging about, and head straight for the bedroom directly across from mine.

"Long time no see," Asher teases when I step into his doorway. He traded in his swim trunks for a pair of basketball shorts, but he's still shirtless, and it's a full-time job to keep my eyes off his defined pecs.

"Lolli and I got caught up talking. And drinking," I say, swallowing a hiccup after my confession.

He chuckles to himself. "That special juice of hers will sneak up on you. You're gonna sleep like a rock tonight."

I fiddle with a strand of hair that's fallen loose from my messy bun as I take another step into his room, pushing the door closed behind me.

His blue eyes narrow to a squint. "Is everything okay, Bailey?"

Pulling in a deep breath and harnessing the power of liquid courage, I close the distance between us and press my palm against his chest. *Yup.* There's that buzz in my fingertips again.

"More than okay."

Asher gazes down at my hand, tensing a bit at my touch. His face is so handsome and sculpted and curious.

Curious about this moment. Curious about me. *About us.*

And I am too. I want to know what his lips feel like pressed against mine. I want to know how his tongue tastes when it touches mine. What those huge, calloused hands would feel like moving over my skin.

A slow, shaky exhale escapes his lungs as he places his hands on my waist.

This is it. I'm sure of it.

And then, just as I'm about to do what I've wanted to do for so long, he pulls me tight into a hug, squeezes me once, then lets me go.

"You should go to bed," he says, his voice matter-of-fact.

My brows knit into a tight line born of equal parts disappointment and confusion. "What, you don't want to?"

"Of course I want to," he says with a sigh. "I mean, fuck, look at you." His gaze rakes over my curves, a low, quiet growl building in the back of his throat.

"Then what's the problem?"

"The problem is that I can't cross that line with you, Bailey. Not like this."

"Like what?" There's a twinge of annoyance in my voice.

He heaves a sigh. "You've been drinking. And more than that, you're my . . . caretaker. We can discuss this more tomorrow, but right now, we need to get you to bed."

My gaze flicks between Asher and the queen-sized bed behind him. There's more than enough room for the both of us.

"*Your* bed," he says firmly, reading my mind. "Please don't make this any harder than it already is. Come on, I'll meet you in there."

Reluctantly, I sulk off to my bedroom, not bothering to change before slipping underneath the fluffy coral comforter. Asher appears moments later, a tall glass of water in one hand and two aspirin in the other.

"Here. Take these. You'll thank me tomorrow."

I do as I'm told, then finish the glass of water.

"Good girl." He takes the now empty glass, refills it in the bathroom sink, and leaves it on the nightstand "just in case."

"Anything else I can get you?" he asks.

I would respond "a kiss good night" if it weren't for the fact that I'm already half-asleep.

• • •

When I wake up, the sun has already climbed up a good portion of the sky.

I barely made it back to my room last night without falling asleep on my feet. Meaning there's no way I set an alarm. But if my body woke itself up on its own, I know that I've clocked more than my necessary eight hours.

The clock on the bedside table tells me the good news . . . and bad news. It's ten freaking thirty. Which means I got almost eleven hours of sleep.

Holy REM cycle. I haven't slept this many hours straight since before I started med school. During med school, I'd be lucky to get that many hours combined over the course of three days.

Whatever was in Lolli's special juice knocked me on my butt last night and is giving me one hell of a headache this morning. But it's nothing a little aspirin can't fix.

I roll out of bed and reach for my toiletries bag to see if I packed any. Although I'm sure there's some in my medical supplies for Asher if I need backup.

And then the memories start coming back to me.

Asher. The aspirin. His room last night.

Oh no.

My cheeks instantly go hot. Was Lolli's cocktail secretly a love potion? Because I obviously had no self-control last night. Could I really not make it two freaking nights into this trip without coming on to my patient?

I change out of the clothes I fell asleep in and into a fresh pair of denim shorts, a sports bra, and a comfy tee before heading to the bathroom to get ready for the day.

My plan is to swing into Asher's room and apologize before I have to go and face the rest of his family, but when I step into the hall, his door is open and the room is empty. *Shit*. He's up and about already while his medical supervision is too busy sleeping off a hangover. *Just peachy*.

I head to the kitchen, where there's still no sign of Asher, although there is a fresh pot of coffee and plenty of bagels and cream cheese up for grabs. Tess and Steve must have come by early this morning, because she's already finished all the dishes from breakfast and is sitting at the table, sipping on coffee.

"Good morning, Bailey!"

Her voice is cheery, although louder than my hungover self would like. Still, I give her a smile as I pick out a blueberry bagel and pour myself a mug of coffee.

"Have you seen my patient yet this morning?" I ask, taking a seat next to her.

She tilts her head toward the window. Outside, Asher is coaching a game of touch football with his nephews in the sand, giving out instructions on the best way to snap the ball. I guess he's just as good with his nephews as he is with his nieces. It's sweet.

"He's really a sweetheart, you know," Tess says, probably responding to the smile tugging at my lips.

This woman is perceptive. Or maybe I just wear my heart on my sleeve.

I nod. "He's a good guy."

"He's not the wild child the media makes him out to be," she says. "We're all hoping he'll find the right girl who will see through that stuff. Someone who will make him want to settle down." The knowing look she's giving me over her mug nearly makes me choke on my coffee.

"Oh. No," I manage to say between coughs. "I'm not—he isn't—we're just friends. I'm about to start my residency, where they'll be training me to take over as their primary internist in a few years, and . . ."

Tess nods. "You're a busy gal."

"Exactly. Too busy for a relationship, for sure. But—" Then I stop myself before I say, *But not too busy for a hookup.*

Yikes. It's probably not a good idea to let it slip to your patient's mom that you want to ride her son. *My bad.*

"But I'm sure he'll meet the right girl some-day," I say instead. It's a solid save, but she's clear-ly not convinced.

"It always happens when you're not looking," she says, her voice filled with cheer.

But before I can ask her to elaborate on that thought, Asher comes through the sliding glass door, making a beeline for the fridge.

"Good morning, sleepyhead." He grabs a bottle of water and downs it in three long gulps.

Tess takes the opportunity to not so subtly drop an excuse about needing to find Steve, leaving the two of us alone.

Asher grabs a bagel and snags the seat his mom was formerly occupying. "How much of last night do you remember, cutie?"

He's grinning at me, and I suddenly want to die. Like, literally fall into a sinkhole and never be seen again. That would be perfect right about now.

I groan, burying my face in my hands. "All of it, unfortunately. Two of Lolli's cocktails may have made me bold, but my memory is sadly quite intact."

He whistles under his breath. "You had two? One is the limit on those things. Even for me."

"That would've been good to know *before*, Ashe."

"Whoops. Sorry."

I bite into my bagel, buying myself a little time to work up even a fraction of the courage I had last night. There's no putting it off. Might as well jump right in. *Geronimo.*

"Look, we both know I'm the one who should be apologizing. I'm sorry for coming on to you last night. That was really inappropriate of me." My eyes are cast bashfully down at what's left of my coffee as I brace myself for whatever cocky comeback he has in store. Instead, what I get is a snicker.

"You have nothing to apologize for."

Confused, I look up to find him wetting his lower lip with his tongue. It sends a flash of heat through me.

"Let me be clear," he says, his voice quiet but blunt, and his blue eyes filled with amusement. "The only reason I didn't sleep with you last night was because you were drunk. So if you're feeling equally bold tonight, come find me."

Holy shit. Am I delusional? Or did I just hear him right?

I sit, slack jawed and wide eyed, staring at Asher, whose smirk is getting wider by the second. "Are you—are you serious?"

"Serious about what?"

It's not Asher asking. At some point in the last five seconds, Tyson has appeared in the kitchen. He's got his swim trunks on and a bagel in his hand, which he takes an enormous bite of as he blinks at us, waiting for a response.

What is it with this family and interrupting?!

Asher plays it off as gossip about our friend group, which Tyson accepts without further questioning, and moves on to the next topic.

"Mack and I are going paddle boarding. You guys in? We've got four."

"I'm down," Asher says, then turns toward me. "You in?"

"I've never been."

"You'll like it."

"We can teach you," Tyson says. "It's not too hard."

"Will I get wet?"

The smirk returns to Asher's lips. "Oh, you'll be wet. I'll make sure of that."

Tyson scoffs. "I think what this idiot means is, yeah, go get your suit on."

CHAPTER SEVEN

Kiss It Better

Asher

It's our third day here, and I have a phone call with Trey scheduled to start in a few minutes.

Bailey sits at the end of my bed, drinking coffee from a pink polka-dotted mug. Lolli's *favorite* pink polka-dotted mug. It's obvious Bailey's won her over. If she's drinking out of *that* mug, the one I've never been allowed to touch, Lolli's allegiance runs deep already.

It's a little alarming, really.

When we got back from paddle boarding with my cousins, I made a fresh pot of coffee and some eggs for me and Bailey to share. She was quiet as we ate, and it's not like I could probe her for info with my family hovering nearby.

I obviously said way too much when she tried to apologize for coming on to me last night, but I wanted her to know that an apology really wasn't necessary. She's gorgeous, and I'm totally feeling her vibes.

But I don't have time to process all that, because the phone starts ringing, and I accept the call.

"How's my favorite center doing?" Trey asks in lieu of a hello.

"Hey, Trey. Just fine. The headaches are less frequent now, and my strain is actually starting to feel a little better."

"Well, that's certainly positive news."

"Yep. Bailey's here too, if you want to say hello." I hold up my cell, which I've placed on speakerphone.

"Hi, Trey." Bailey moves closer, setting her mug on my nightstand so we can sit together near the phone.

"Hello, young lady. How's our patient been? Not too difficult, I hope."

Bailey looks at me and smiles. "Nothing I can't handle."

"Good to hear. How's the strain coming along?"

Bailey looks at me, waiting for me to show her my injury so that she can respond to Trey. Since the first day we arrived and she tended to me in the sunroom, I've avoided those deft fingers getting too close, well, to all the important parts, again, so she hasn't actually seen it in the last couple of days.

"Let me just examine him," Bailey says, ending the long pause in conversation. "May I take a look?" she asks me, her voice lower.

"Have at it," I mutter.

I lean back on the bed, propped up on my elbows, and watch as she hikes up the right leg of my shorts, running a warm palm up the expanse of my thigh. I suck in a ragged inhale when she moves my boxers to the side next, careful not to expose more of me than she should.

The deep purple color of the bruising has faded into pinks and lavenders. I can't help but see the concern written all over Bailey's face as she gazes down at my injury.

"Is the swelling down?" Trey asks.

"In a manner of speaking," I say, feeling slightly dizzy.

It doesn't take a medical degree to know a different part of my anatomy is currently swelling for an entirely different reason. Thankfully, Bailey doesn't seem to notice, or she's hella good at pretending she doesn't notice.

"Keep up the ice regimen and call me right away if anything changes."

"Absolutely," I manage to say.

When I finally look up, I find Bailey's eyes are clear and bright and kind. She likes this, being here. Helping me. Looking after my aches and bruised muscles. I like it too—way too much.

"Feel better, bro," a deep masculine voice calls from the background.

Trey clears his throat. "That was Landon. I'm taping up his wrist."

"Ah, tell him thanks and will do," I say.

There are a few more shouts and well-wishes from a couple of the guys on my team in the background, which leave me smiling as we end the call.

Bailey is watching me curiously, like she's trying to piece something together. I wait her out, knowing she's got something on her mind.

Finally, she says, "This must be so different for you—being here, surrounded by all these women instead of the testosterone-fueled locker-room talk you're used to."

"Yeah. A little, I guess. But this is how I grew up, so it's normal for me. I'm fine with a little girl talk."

She smiles. "I could see that."

"Plus, I actually hate gender stereotypes."

"You?" Bailey's tone is filled with shock. "You're the manliest man I know, Mister Star Athlete. Mister Tough-as-Nails Hockey Player."

It's funny to know that's how she sees me. "Eh. Maybe? But, shit, I would happily stay home and cook and clean all day, and have a wife who's the breadwinner."

"Hmm." She considers this, still watching me.

"And if I want to cry at the song 'Over the Rainbow', that should be totally acceptable."

She softens, leaning one arm on the bed beside me. "You're right. It should. It's a very beautiful song."

"Damn straight it is. As a man, we're practically taught that it's not okay to show our feelings and emotions."

"True, I never thought about it that way," Bailey says quietly. She still hasn't moved from her spot beside me on the bed.

"Hey, thanks for being here. For all this. For looking after me."

Her lips part and she shifts her weight, so she's leaning the slightest bit closer. "It's really no hardship."

When I place my hand on top of hers, she doesn't pull it away like I half expect her to. "Still. I appreciate it." My voice has gone husky, and I can't deny that we're sharing some type of moment.

It seems like all the chemistry between us that I've been trying to deny, all those heated stares over the last few days, rush to the surface. I lean in, and so does Bailey, until she's close enough that I can press my mouth to hers. A small gasp of surprise parts her lips, and I use it to my advantage, sucking her plump lower lip between mine and deepening our kiss.

She kisses me back with skill and certainty, the certainty that *yes*, we should absolutely be kissing right now. Like nothing else matters in this moment except for the stroking of her tongue against mine. And, *oh my fucking God*, it's perfect. Her mouth fits seamlessly against mine, and I swallow a low groan when I feel her fingers thread into the hair at the back of my neck.

I tell myself this kiss has nothing to do with the things I overheard my douchey cousins whisper when Bailey came out in her bathing suit. It has nothing to do with her adorably drunken come-on last night. I just wanted to kiss her.

And the kiss doesn't disappoint.

She's breathing hard now, and her thighs press together as I imagine there's an ache building between them. An ache I'd be more than happy to tend to. Well, that is, if I were able to, but fuck it, I'd risk sitting out the rest of the season if I meant I could have Bailey. But that dangerous thought is interrupted by the sound of footsteps thudding up the stairs. We pull apart just in time.

My mother appears in the doorway.

I'm breathing hard and my cock is standing in a full salute, but my mother is so distracted, she doesn't notice.

"Nora's water broke!"

Mom's out of breath like she ran all the way here. And maybe she did. My oldest sister and her husband are staying at my mom's house, which is a couple of streets over. "They're on their way to the hospital."

I jump up from the bed, making a quick adjustment, and rush over to her. "Holy shit. Are you serious?"

"It's time!" she says happily, unable to wipe the huge smile from her face.

I turn to Bailey, who's now standing too, also smiling. "Should we go? We should go to the hospital, right?"

Mom pats my shoulder. "Babies take time. Take a shower and get something to eat, then come up a bit later."

I nod. "Okay. I can do that."

My heart is pounding hard. I'm not sure if it's because I was just kissing Bailey, or because my mother almost caught us, or because my sister has just gone into labor. Probably a combination of all three.

My mom bounds back down the stairs with excitement, and Bailey steps into the hall after her.

"I'll shower and get ready quickly. This is so exciting."

I want to kiss her again, but instead I just nod. "Meet you downstairs?"

She gives me one last appraising look, and then disappears toward her bedroom.

• • •

We've been stationed in the waiting room of the obstetrics wing of the hospital for going on five hours now. Courtney and Amber are playing a card game at the other end of the room. My mom is sitting with Steve on a love seat, and Lolli left two hours ago to go to bed. Bailey is sitting in a chair beside me, fiddling with some word-search game on her phone.

The last update we got from Nora's doctor was that it would probably be another couple of hours until the baby is here.

I stretch and look down at my phone for the time—almost midnight. I guess my mom was right—babies take time, especially first babies. I can't help the nervous knot forming in my stomach as I worry about Nora. I hope she's okay. But they'd tell us if there was anything abnormal, right?

Turning toward Bailey, I extend my legs out in front of me and bring one arm around the back of her chair. "It's late. You should get out of here. At least one of us should get some sleep."

Bailey's gaze meets mine with a playful look. "And miss all this free hospital coffee? No way."

I chuckle. "Have it your way."

She looks around, her eyes smiling. "It's actually pretty cushy for a hospital waiting room."

I shrug. "That's California for you."

Neither of us has mentioned it, but I can't stop thinking about that kiss. Can't stop replaying the eager way her tongue met mine, or the feel of her fingers threading into my hair. The thought of it gives me chills on the back of my neck even now, hours later.

Another hour slips by, and I think I doze off for a few minutes, as uncomfortable as it is folding my lanky frame into a stiff waiting-room chair, I somehow manage to sleep. But when my mother bursts through the doors and I'm suddenly wide awake. She's just come from visiting Nora's room.

"It's almost time!" Mom's practically vibrating with excitement. "I just got kicked out because

Nora has started to push."

I look to Bailey, whose eyes are wide and not the least bit bleary. Maybe she's used to pulling all-night hospital rotations, because this doesn't seem to be affecting her like it is me.

"What does that mean? That the baby's almost here?" I ask.

Bailey tilts her chin, considering how to answer my question. "As a first-time mom, pushing can take anywhere from twenty minutes to three hours, unfortunately."

"Come on, Nora," I say in a quiet cheer, and Bailey gives my hand a squeeze in silent support.

Thankfully, it's only about forty-five minutes later when my sister's husband, Todd, bursts through the doors, breathless and with a huge smile on his face. Mom jumps up from her seat, then we all do, crowding around him.

"It's a girl!" His voice is filled with such reverence as he says this, and his eyes are a little watery.

Mom immediately breaks down in tears. "Another little girl," she says softly, tears now sliding down both cheeks.

"Seven pounds, one ounce." Todd huffs out

each word like he's just run a marathon.

"And Nora?" I ask.

"Nora's great. She did amazing."

We all take turns looking at the couple of blurry pictures he managed to snag with his phone—my tiny, splotchy pink niece lying naked in a bassinet, her mouth open in a wailing cry. Her swaddled and resting peacefully on Nora's chest as they gaze at each other.

A lump lodges itself in my throat.

Bailey touches my shoulder, her warm palm sliding over it. "Congratulations, Uncle Ashe. You okay?" she asks softly when she meets my gaze.

I sniff and rub my eyes. "Yeah. Just something wrong with my damn eye." As I wipe it again, Bailey's knowing smile is sweet and not the least bit mocking.

"I'd better get back in there," Todd says, pocketing his phone.

"Congratulations, Daddy!" Courtney calls after him.

By the time Nora is transferred from the birthing suite to a maternity room, it's the wee hours of the morning, and we all leave to head back to the house. It's pitch-black outside and cool in the parking lot, and when I see Bailey shiver, I wrap one arm around her, guiding her to the bright yellow convertible.

When we reach the house, Lolli is still up and has a stack of warm pancakes waiting for us, along with crisp bacon and orange juice.

I groan when I see the spread. "Lolli, you're fucking amazing."

She sighs and shakes a spatula at me. "That mouth is going to get you in trouble."

Bailey throws me a cautious look from across the table, her mouth twisted in a wry smirk. Suddenly, I want to show her just how much trouble I could get into with my mouth, and preferably, as soon as possible. Instead, I settle for a large stack of pancakes and six strips of bacon while Lolli demands information about the new baby.

We tell her everything we know, which isn't all that much, then finish eating in exhausted silence. Even Bailey, who was so chipper at the hospital, is slumped over in her seat. She takes a few bites of her food and then rinses her plate before placing it in the dishwasher. Lolli shoos her away from the sink before she can do any more.

"Thank you, Lolli. Love you," I say with a press of my lips to her cheek. "Sorry for cursing, it's just . . . *bacon*. It brings out the cave man in me."

"I understand," she says, taking my plate and glass from me to load them into the dishwasher.

My sisters have already disappeared upstairs, and Bailey is looking sleepier by the second.

"Come on," I say, putting my arm around her shoulders. "Let's go get some rest."

"See you all in the morning," Lolli calls.

I don't point out the fact that it's already morning. Hopefully, we can all sleep late.

• • •

And that's exactly what happens, because after I say good night to Bailey and brush my teeth, the next thing I know, it's noon and I'm waking up to a sun-filled bedroom. The house is totally quiet as I make my way downstairs in search of coffee.

Turns out, there isn't any. And there's no one in the house either, which is strange. Bailey's bedroom door was open and the room was empty when I passed by. I work on making a pot of coffee for myself since I apparently missed the breakfast rush.

A lot happened yesterday, and as I wait for the coffee to brew, I can't help but re-examine it all. That kiss I shared with Bailey was fucking perfect, and then becoming an uncle and watching Bailey's joy, and seeing how well she fit in with my family . . . it's a lot to take in. Maybe it's the lack of sleep, but I'm feeling emotional, like I'm the one who had pregnancy hormones or some shit. Speaking of, I wonder how Nora and the baby are doing this morning.

The sound of laughter interrupts my thoughts, and I wander to the windows with a mug of steaming coffee and peer outside. Bailey is out on the sand, lying on a beach towel between Courtney and Amber. She's wearing that pink two-piece bathing suit I saw her put into the dresser drawer our first night here, and my first thought is *damn*.

Soft, pale, creamy skin. Cleavage I want to bury my face in, and so many delicious curves I want to discover over and over again.

They're laughing about something, cracking up, and Bailey pushes her sunglasses up to wipe tears from her eyes before flopping down onto the towel again. She looks so small next to my sisters, who have both always been on the taller side.

A stiff wind would blow her over. We're no match physically. So, why is that so appealing?

The idea of protecting Bailey and being the one to care for her is intriguing to me. Maybe it's because she's been looking after me these last few days? I'm not even sure that makes sense, but it's the only explanation I've got.

"Whatcha doing?"

Lolli's voice from behind me makes me jump. I turn and force a smile. "Nothing much."

I take another sip of coffee as Lolli peers around me to look out the windows. Then she makes a knowing sound and smiles at me.

"Mm-hmm. Why don't you get your suit on and go out there?"

I don't think that's a very good idea—not with Bailey out there looking like a fucking snack.

"I'd prefer to stay in. You have anything you need help with?" I ask, hope in my tone.

Lolli shakes her head. "I'm good."

"Any light bulbs that need to be changed?"

She gives me a blank stare. "I said I'm good."

What does she not understand about this? I need something to occupy me. Something other than the images running rampant through my brain about getting up close and personal with Bailey's curves.

"Any laundry I could do for you?" There are six people staying in this house. Surely, there are towels and sheets to wash.

Lolli purses her lips and gives her head another shake. "Now I know something's up if you're volunteering to do laundry. This wouldn't have anything to do with that gorgeous girl out there in her bikini, would it?"

"'Bye, Lolli," I grumble.

After refilling my mug, I take my coffee upstairs to sulk in peace while Lolli stands in the kitchen, grinning at me like she knows something I don't.

As I'm walking away I hear her mumble something about me taking one too many pucks to the head.

CHAPTER EIGHT

Nacho Average Goose Bumps

Bailey

This morning, for the first time since we arrived, the house is quiet.

It was late morning when I woke up. My internal clock is out of whack from our late night at the hospital, but it was totally worth it to see the look of pride and love that covered Asher's face when it was announced that he had a new baby niece. He's such a softie when it comes to his family, that much is obvious.

For the past few days, there has been no shortage of noise in this house, regardless of the time of day. So, when Amber, Courtney, and I come in from the beach to a mostly silent house, it's actually a little unsettling. Tess and Steve are hosting some of the other family members at their house, and as for Lolli, there's a light pink sticky note on the counter that says she's making a grocery run. But that leaves one very important person unaccounted for.

"Has anyone seen Asher?" I ask, pulling my denim shorts from my beach bag and shimmying them up my legs. I'm a little self-conscious in just my strappy pink bikini now that we're not on the beach, but Courtney and Amber show no signs of changing out of their respective tankini and one-piece suits, so neither will I.

Amber shrugs as she hoists herself up onto the kitchen counter, her legs dangling off the side. "If he's still asleep, I'm going to give him so much shit." The second the curse word slips out, she slaps a hand over her mouth, only to peel it away when she remembers that there are no young ears in the house. "Phew. It's nice to be able to let a few swear words slip. I'm not used to being around kids and having to watch my mouth all the time."

"Welcome to the life of a teacher," Courtney says teasingly, referring to her own line of work. "Speaking of which, my kiddos usually eat at noon, and so do I, so I'm famished. What do we have in the way of lunch supplies?"

One look in the refrigerator, and I immediately

see why Lolli ran out to get groceries. The fridge is looking more than a little empty after three full days of feeding a small army.

"It looks like we're doing leftovers," I say, scanning the shelves of plastic leftover mystery containers and condiments. "Unless anyone is in the mood for pickle spears dipped in hot sauce. Because that's about all we have."

"We could always just wait until Lolli gets home," Amber says.

Courtney widens her eyes hopefully. "Or we could pick up something on our way to visit Nora at the hospital."

Amber shakes her head and taps her blank phone screen. "No visiting Nora until we get the go-ahead from Todd. We don't want to step on any toes. Which is why we should just wait it out until Lolli gets home with food. We can all eat lunch together, and maybe by then we'll have news on Nora or the go-ahead to visit them at the hospital for a visit."

It's a sensible plan, but the enormous rumble that comes from Amber's stomach mid-sentence is evidence that that plan is not going to work.

Cue the three of us going full search mission on

the kitchen.

Courtney takes the pantry while Amber and I cover the fridge and freezer. Between the three of us, we come up with most of a block of cheddar cheese left over from burgers, a Tupperware container of sloppy-joe meat, and a plastic bag of cold pancakes, courtesy of Lolli's late-night cooking session. Quite the assortment.

"Bingo! Look what I found." Courtney pulls her head out of the back of the pantry and proudly holds up half a bag of tortilla chips. "And, bonus points, they aren't even expired!"

"Soooo, nachos?" I say, grabbing the block of cheddar off the counter.

Amber, who is still petitioning that we wait for Lolli to get back with groceries, is the first to poke a hole in my nacho plan. "What about protein?"

Courtney folds her arms with a huff. "Leave it to you to worry about a well-balanced meal when we're two seconds away from wrapping a hot dog in a pancake and calling it lunch."

I laugh while secretly making a mental note to try that out sometime. Pancakes and hot dogs? That sounds like the best PMS food ever.

"What about the sloppy-joe meat? Could barbeque nachos be a thing?"

Courtney looks at me like I've just solved world hunger. "That might be an actual stroke of genius. What do you think, Amber? Yay or nay?"

The skeptical look on Amber's face quickly fades into a curious smile. "Is it bad if that actually sounds kind of good?"

"Nope." I laugh. "Sounds like a good thing to me. Because that's exactly what's on the menu."

Never underestimate the power of three hangry women, because with a little teamwork and a lot of cheese-based motivation, we have a full tray of nachos prepped in no time. After a few minutes in the oven, we have an end product that slightly resembles a failed seventh grade science project. A very messy, very delicious-looking failed science project that I can't wait to dig into.

We don't even bother to divide it onto plates, opting instead to put the baking sheet of nachos in the middle of the kitchen island for easy sharing. It reminds me of the sleepovers I used to have with friends growing up, where we used to share pepperoni pizzas or trays of brownies. As we each pull a chip from the cheesy barbecue mess, I feel just like a kid again.

Courtney lets out a guttural moan as she chews. "Oh my God. These are amazing. We need to have these every summer."

I turn to Amber to ask what she thinks, but the fact that she already has a chip in each hand says it all.

It looks like we've officially started a new tradition of barbeque nachos at Lolli's house, and I can't help but smile knowing that, with all this family has given me this week, I've made some small contribution, and a connection that feels really genuine.

After a few more chips, we decide that we need to have Lolli pick up more tortilla chips and sloppy-joe meat so that the rest of the family can try our new creation. Amber grabs her phone to give Lolli a call, but based on the way her brows shoot up her forehead when she looks at her phone screen, I'm guessing we finally got an update on Nora.

"Baby news?" Courtney asks, crossing her fingers with both hands.

Amber nods, holding up a finger as she finishes chewing. "It's Todd. He says that Nora and the baby are doing well, but they'll both be in the hospital for a few more days yet."

"A few days?" Courtney chews worriedly at her lower lip. "Is that normal?"

"It's totally normal for a slightly early delivery," I explain, hoping my calm will rub off on her. "And since this is Nora's first baby, a little extra time to recover is normal too. It sounds like both mom and baby are going to be just fine."

"Did he say anything about us visiting, though?" Courtney's gaze darts between Amber and me, looking for an answer that neither of us has.

Amber's fingers fly across her keyboard. Moments later, she has a response. "Nora can accept visitors anytime before four, but Todd says she's resting right now. So, maybe in like an hour?"

"That would give us time to pick up a present for the new mom," I say.

We launch into a brainstorming session of what Nora might want, agreeing that an assortment of things would probably be best. Just as Courtney hits the button to confirm our online purchase for in-store pickup, a soft thudding of steps comes down the stairs, and our girl time is officially over.

"Well, look who decided to finally get out of bed," Amber teases.

Asher is standing in the doorway in swim trunks and a well-worn Ice Hawks tee, his hair freshly washed. And, suddenly, I'm thinking about him naked in the shower, the water beading down those six-pack abs, his arms flexing as he massages shampoo into his hair. Him lathering up his—

Ugh. I've been turned on nonstop since our mini make-out session got interrupted yesterday. Granted, it was interrupted by the birth of his niece, which is about a million times more important than us getting handsy, but still. Try telling that to the desperate ache between my thighs.

It didn't help that seeing him get all emotional in the hospital waiting room tugged at my heart-strings and hormones. Now, knowing that the house is practically empty, it's taking a lot of willpower not to drag Asher's freshly showered body back up those stairs and into his bedroom.

Double ugh. He's the one with the concussion, not me, so why am I the one not thinking straight?

"Really? Now that I'm ready to join you guys on the beach, you're all inside?" Asher grabs a chip off the tray of nachos and pops the whole thing in his mouth at once, scrunching his brow in thought as he chews. "Did you guys put sloppy-joe meat on nachos?"

"One question at a time, hotshot," Amber says with an eye roll. "Which of those do you want answered first?"

He huffs out a soft laugh, wiping his mouth with the back of his hand. "Actually, new question. Do you think Nora's up for visitors yet? I swear I've been checking my phone every five minutes waiting for updates."

"Way ahead of you, bro. I've got all the details right here," Amber brags, tapping her phone screen. "Todd texted me to say Nora and the baby will be in for a few days yet, but she's accepting visitors before four. And your girl, Bailey, is a genius who came up with not only the nacho creation, but also the best presents ever to take to Nora and the baby."

Amber's word choice sends goose bumps up and down my arms. *Your girl, Bailey.* I like the sound of that a little too much.

"You can make these for me anytime you want, Bailey." Asher snags another nacho while raising a brow in my direction. "What'd you come up with for a present?"

"Well, Amber and Courtney were talking about how Nora is super addicted to trail mix," I say with a smile. "And since new moms need extra calories when nursing, we're going to pick out some fancy trail mixes at a foodie boutique and put it in a basket with a pair of slippers and a couple of other little things."

"We already found a great pair online that's available for pickup." Courtney flips her phone toward Asher to show him the fluffy memory foam slippers we've already paid for online. "See? Bailey picked them out because they're sunshine yellow."

"Her favorite color," Asher mutters under his breath before turning his attention back to me. "You knew that already?"

I'm not sure if he's impressed or weirded out that I remembered such a minor detail about his sister, so I wave it off. "It's no big deal. I just want her to feel special. All the attention shifts to the baby after its born, so the mom often gets forgotten about, if you know what I mean."

Asher's eyes deepen to a darker, more serious blue, his lips parting ever so slightly in the softest, subtlest smile. "I think you make a lot of people feel special, Bailey."

Remember those goose bumps on my arms? Yeah, well, now they're everywhere. And these aren't just your average goose bumps. These are the kind of goose bumps that make your whole body tingle and your toes grip the kitchen tile. These are next level. They send you straight to cloud nine.

We do a little more damage on the nachos before Courtney and Amber head upstairs to rinse off and get ready, leaving Asher and me alone for the first time since last night.

"So, you're getting my sister a present before I do, huh?" Asher rakes his fingers through his hair, giving me one of those amused half smiles he's so famous for.

I can't look him in the eye without turning pink. "I hope I'm not overstepping," I say, directing it more at my toes than to Asher. "Maybe it's weird for Nora to get a present from me since I hardly know her."

"You're not overstepping. You're being thoughtful. I can't believe you knew her favorite color already."

I shrug, chewing my lower lip as I shift my

gaze to meet his. "I try to remember details. Plus, I really like your sisters."

"They seem to really like you too." He props his forearms on the kitchen island, giving me a world-class view of the thick veins running up them, then leans in until we're close enough that I can feel his breath on my skin. "But not as much as I do. Which is why I think you should come by my room tonight."

His voice is low and teasing. But I'm 100 percent up for the challenge.

"Maybe I will," I say once I find my breath, my voice quivering ever so slightly.

Is he going to kiss me? Is he going to lift me onto this island and press his mouth to mine right here, right now?

Instead, he takes one thumb and presses it gently against my lower lip as his tongue sweeps over his own. "Can't wait, cutie."

He shoots me a wink, then pulls away, sauntering toward the sliding glass door. Just like that. As if he hadn't just left me hot and heavy in his wake.

But as he tugs the door open, he pauses, looking over his shoulder, his eyes glittering with trouble.

"Do you happen to know what my favorite color is?"

I shake my head. "What is it?"

"As of today?" His gaze wanders from mine, tracing the curve of my shoulder and landing on the cups of my bikini top. "Pink. And it has absolutely nothing to do with my new niece, by the way."

CHAPTER NINE

Sorry, Not Sorry

Asher

"**K**nock, knock," a female voice calls softly from the hall.

I pull open the door to my bedroom and am met with the sight of Bailey standing in front of me, dressed in a gauzy white sundress, her feet bare. "Hey."

Her eyes meet mine as she stammers out a barely audible *hi*, and then her gaze tracks hotly down my naked torso, lingering over my chest muscles and abs. A pink tinge spreads over her cheeks.

Bingo.

I knew she was due back soon, and she'd promised to check in on me. My sisters had texted photos from their visit at the hospital. The fact that I'm shirtless and fresh out of the shower is a total co-incidence.

Yeah, right. Hashtag Sorry Not Sorry.

I might be playing with fire, but fuck it, I'm too far gone to care. I want her. And if I'm being honest, I always did. I just figured she was too good for me—she's a smart, career-driven woman. I'm known for one-night stands and casual hookups.

But seeing her here, in my space, with my family, it's changing things. Making me want things, things I never thought I'd want.

It's not that I'm allergic to monogamy. It's just I've never seen the point—never met a person I wanted to lock down as badly as I do Bailey. She's honestly the first woman I've ever pictured myself in a relationship with.

"Is now still a good time?" she asks, the color on her cheeks deepening. Has she been reliving that kiss like I have?

"Of course. Come on in."

She steps around me and into the room, and I close the door behind her.

It's then I notice that she's carrying a couple of the instant cold packs Trey had stocked her up with before we left the training facility.

She holds one up. "Figured it was time for one of these."

I nod. "Sure." I wait for her to hand it to me, but she doesn't. So I sit down on the side of the bed and straighten my right leg out in front of me. "You want to do the honors?" I ask when I realize she still hasn't moved from her spot at the edge of the bed.

"Right." She nods like she's suddenly remembering what we're doing here.

It's okay. You can look at my six-pack anytime you want, sweetheart.

Just when I'm considering if there's a chill way I could make a joke about her kissing all my boo-boos, Bailey launches into a story about today, about something funny Courtney said, and then visiting Nora and the baby, and how she and Amber realized they both hate yoga.

Honestly, I should be paying better attention, but all I can focus on is the thought of the soft pads of her fingers as they stroke over my bruised skin, inching ever closer to my stiffening cock. She smells so good, like sunshine and shampoo, and my mood is immediately lifted when she takes a seat on the bed beside me. Then she hikes up my shorts to expose the tender spot.

The truth is, she's freaking perfect. And that scares the hell out of me. No girl is perfect, right? Except to me, Bailey is. She's stunning. Funny. Smart. Driven. Educated. I should stop tallying this mental list, and I do, because Bailey is directing those gorgeous dark eyes my way again.

"Any other symptoms I should know about?" she asks, looking down like she's pleased with my recovery so far.

"Nothing that you kissing me won't cure," I say, curling one hand against the back of her neck to urge her forward.

She comes willingly and rewards me with a slow, sweet kiss. It's perfection.

If I thought kissing her the last time was perfect, today is on a whole new level. There's familiarity now, and a level of skill I couldn't appreciate last time in my over-excitement. When her lips part, I slide my tongue against hers, and Bailey shivers.

Then she does something I don't expect at all. She places her palms flat against my chest and pushes until I lie back, and she crawls right into my waiting lap, straddling me.

Fuck yeah.

I cup her ass in my hands as my tongue flirts with hers. I'm fully hard now, and Bailey rocks herself against the firm ridge in my shorts. My entire body shudders at how good that feels. Her movements knock the ice pack out of place, and it rolls next to my thigh, the cold startling me. I toss it across the room and keep right on kissing her.

"This okay?" I ask when she pulls her lips from mine.

"Less talking. More kissing," she says, diving back in for more.

I groan, long and low in my throat, when she rocks against me. Her dress has ridden up her parted thighs, and I can feel the warmth between her legs as she presses against me.

Part of me wants to ask her what we're doing, and if she's sure she's okay with this. In all the years I've known her, we've never ventured outside the friend zone. But the other part of me, the hornier part, tells me to shut the hell up and enjoy the moment.

Her hips shift restlessly on top of me, and I let out a long groan. "Fuck, Bailey. You feel so good."

"Touch me." She breathes out the words, rocking her hips against me more firmly.

"Happily, sweetheart."

I place one more soft kiss on her mouth and then my lips move lower, tracing the pulse in her throat, then nibble at her collarbone as I pull down the top of her dress and work my way toward the generous swell of her breasts. They are more than a handful.

"Fuck, I'm the luckiest man alive right now."

She chuckles for a moment, but the sound quickly turns to gasps as I tease one perky nipple with my tongue.

"Or do you do this with all your patients?"

She pulls back, and I immediately regret the thoughtless words that left my mouth. *Way to be a fucking dipshit, Asher.*

Her body tensing in my hold, she says, "You're right. This is totally unprofessional."

"Bailey, I'm kidding. I know you would never. Forgive me for being an idiot? I'm going to blame it on the blood flow that's all been diverted south."

She twists her lips—it's almost a smile—and

shakes her head at me.

"We're both adults. If you want to stop, then that's exactly what we'll do, but if you want to keep going, I would love to make you come on my tongue. Or my fingers. Or my cock." *Or all three . . .*

She kisses me again, and I smile against her mouth. I'm so happy.

"That what you want too?" I ask.

"Yes . . ."

When she hesitates like there's something more on her mind, I ask, "But?"

She chews on her lower lip for a second as her gaze flicks up to the door. It doesn't have a lock, unfortunately, and I think Bailey's just realized that.

"What if someone comes in? Maybe we shouldn't get naked."

I'd like to assure her that Lolli wouldn't just barge in without knocking first, but let's be honest. My grandmother does a lot of things I wouldn't expect her to. Like mechanical bull riding.

"I can work with that," I say, nuzzling her

breasts again. I'm a little obsessed with these, apparently.

I lift Bailey off of me and place her carefully in the center of the bed. Then I crawl down her body until I'm eye level with the lace of her panties. Her dress is rucked up just enough, and I plant one hand on the soft skin of her stomach, and move her panties to the side with the other.

Bailey trembles when my tongue touches her clit.

With lazy flicks of my tongue, I tease her until she's dragging her fingers through my hair and making soft, need-filled whimpers. She tastes so good, and her body is so responsive to every lick and nibble. When I seal my lips to her and suck, her hips shoot up off the bed. After a few minutes more, Bailey comes apart, gasping and quivering against me.

She's breathless when I lie down beside her.

"That was so hot," I say, grinning at her.

"Don't get too cocky," she says, but she's smiling too.

God, this feels so right—her and me. I chuckle and turn her lips to mine so I can press one more kiss to her perfect mouth.

"What about …" She looks down at the eager erection tenting the front of my pants. "Should I…?"

Just the thought of her touching me has me ready to explode. "I'll take care of it later," I say, kissing her again.

Bailey adjusts her panties and tugs down the skirt of her dress. "Well, that was fun," she says, still slightly breathless.

"I'm here all week," I joke.

She shakes her head, watching me with a soft expression. "Don't worry, Ashe. I know it's just a week. I'm not looking for a relationship."

"You're not?"

She laughs. "God, no. I'm just about to enter one of the busiest times of my life. I'll hardly have time to even sleep, let alone tend to another human being."

"Right," I grit out. "Of course." The words feel like sandpaper in my throat.

A few minutes later, after Bailey has repositioned the ice pack against me, she gives me one last kiss and then pauses at the door. "Ice that for at least twenty minutes. See ya downstairs later, right?"

"Don't eat all the snickerdoodles," I say, smiling.

But inside, my chest is tight. I feel like someone just dropped a bomb on me, and I have no idea why I'd feel anything but incredible right now. I just pleasured a gorgeous girl, a girl who takes care of me, and who gets along with my family. I should feel like the king of the freaking world right now, not like a sorry lump of shit.

With a deep sigh, I shove a pillow under my head and close my eyes, trying to figure out what the hell just happened, and why the thought of Bailey not wanting a relationship makes me feel so grumpy.

CHAPTER TEN

A Watched Phone Never Rings

Bailey

It's 10:55 a.m. and I'm sitting cross-legged in the middle of my bed, wondering if staring at the time on my phone will make it move faster.

I need it to be 11:00 a.m., a.k.a. the start of Aubree's lunch break. I texted her this morning, telling her I need to talk, not just text. Because if I don't tell someone about what happened with Asher last night, I think I may actually explode.

Or let it slip in conversation with his sisters, or in front of his family. Which, frankly, would be way worse, and I'd possibly die of embarrassment and humiliation.

At breakfast this morning, I'm pretty sure I visibly flinched every time anyone said "come" or "down" or any other word that my brain could twist into an innuendo about what Asher and I did last night. And when he met my eyes from across the breakfast table, smirking with his lips around a forkful of eggs, the mischievous blue depths of his eyes hinted at his indecent thoughts.

I wished I could extract every single one of them like a suture from an incision, but no such luck. Which was for the best, because I doubt my own impure thoughts would have been as easily concealed. My face threatened to turn as red as a tomato at the idea of getting him naked. That's not a fact I need his grandmother aware of, no matter how close I've grown to her this week.

The final nail in the coffin was when Lolli made a comment about how Asher is "such a big eater." I just about spit cereal across the table. Hence, me hiding out in my room right now, instead of running to the store with Lolli and Tess to get party supplies. I've put myself in time-out until I no longer feel like I'm wearing a sign on my forehead that reads **ASK ME ABOUT ASHER'S IMPRESSIVE ORAL SEX SKILLS**.

My thumb hovers over Aubree's contact as I watch the clock roll over from 10:59 to 11:00, and then I tap the **CALL** button the instant it does.

Should I probably have waited for her to call

me? Yeah. But do I have the patience for that? Nope. Not even a little. It rings a few times, but just when it's about to go to voicemail, she picks up.

Thank freaking God.

"Hi, I'm wrapping up a few things, so please disregard any background noise."

Aubree has her own office at the organization where she works doing Ice Hawks' philanthropy work, which affords this conversation a little privacy. And since Asher left to visit Nora and the baby right after breakfast, I don't have to worry about him overhearing anything through the bedroom wall.

"How's work?" I ask, trying to regulate my heart rate and keep the conversation normal.

She groans in response. "Ask me again once gala season is over." I can practically hear her eye roll through the phone over the sound of her shuffling papers. "How's California?"

Amazing. Orgasmic. Thrilling. "It's actually been really good."

"That's awesome. God, I'm so over this gala. If my boss asks me to change the seating chart one more time . . ." She huffs out a frustrated exhale.

"Please talk to me about sandy beaches or tropical drinks or something. Anything to remind me that there's life beyond this spreadsheet of donors."

I suck in a deep breath, weighing my words. I may as well just come right out and say it. Ripping off the Band-Aid in three . . . two . . . one . . .

"I hooked up with Asher."

"Oh my God, you didn't!" She lets out an excited squeal.

My heart speeds up at the memory of the way Asher's blue eyes clouded over with lust, at the way he kissed a path down my body . . . at the way he feasted on me like I was the best thing he's ever tasted. *Gah!* My belly flips even now.

"I did." At those two words, I have to pull the phone away from my ear briefly or risk being deafened by Aubree's high-pitched squeals.

"Damn, woman!"

I chuckle. "I know. I wasn't expecting anything like that when I agreed to come on this trip, but there's just this connection between us that's intensified over the last few days. And, I mean, you have eyeballs. You've seen the guy."

I don't want to admit it to her, but aside from

just how gorgeous he is, watching him help his grandma with little tasks, seeing him get emotional about the birth of his new niece . . . I don't know. I guess it sort of changed the way I look at him.

But I meant what I said to him—this is only for the week. I have no expectations that this will turn into something more. And, frankly, I don't want it to. I need to be 100-percent focused on my career. Plus, Asher Reed is a total playboy, and I'm under no illusions that I'm the woman who will change his playboy ways, let alone be the woman he settles down with.

"He is fine as fuck," Aubree says, agreeing with me. "What was it like?"

"It was good."

I almost laugh at my own word choice. *Good* is much too tame a word for what we shared, but I'm unsure what else to say. Plus, I'm being hit with a sudden wave of modesty. The man is a giver, but I'm not sure I should divulge that piece of information to Aubree.

"Dude, you're not getting off that easily. Well, apparently you did get off that easily." She cracks up at her own joke. "Seriously, Bailey, sisters before misters!" she shouts into the phone.

Smiling, I shake my head, wondering what her coworkers are thinking about her random outbursts. "Fine. You get one question."

"Hmm." She ponders this for what feels like an hour. "And you'll answer whatever I ask honestly?"

Nerves flutter in my belly. "Of course, I will."

There's silence on the other end of the line for a second, and then Aubree clears her throat. "Okay. My question is . . . what was his dick like?"

I burst into laughter at her unexpected and rather inappropriate question. "I have no idea. I didn't see it."

Her gasp of disbelief filters through the phone. "What exactly did this hookup involve then?"

I guess I'm not going to get by without divulging some details. I take a deep breath and stammer, "He, um . . . went downstairs."

Aubree cheers. "Yes! But, wait . . . that was all?"

"What do you mean?"

"You didn't do anything to him in return? A quid pro quo, if you will."

I laugh. "Um, no, but he's injured. Five minutes before that, I was examining him and icing down his groin."

"True. But *still*. Wait a minute, it still works, right?"

"Yes, it still works, at least what I felt when I was straddling him tells me all systems were a go. What do you mean by but *still*?" I ask, confused. I'm smart enough to know that when a sexy-as-hell man wants to go down on you, you let him. Full stop.

"Just saying, you're a badass woman. I think I want to be you when I grow up."

This sends me into a fit of laughter, because at thirty and the director of a charity organization, Aubree is a badass herself, and most definitely a grown-up.

But then I'm struck by a sudden thought. Maybe I was selfish.

Asher didn't seem upset, didn't seem concerned with anything other than my pleasure, so I guess I won't overthink it. And who knows? He seems to be healing nicely, so maybe he'll get lucky and I'll have a chance to return the favor before the week's end. Maybe then I'll be able to answer Aubree's question about his package.

"Okay, I get a new question since you couldn't answer my first one," Aubree says firmly. Apparently, she's making the rules now. "Isn't his entire family in the same house as you guys? How did you pull off a . . . what did you call it? Trip downstairs?"

I lower my voice a few decibels at the reminder. Even with Asher visiting Nora, there are still plenty of other ears that could be listening in.

"We had to get a little creative," I murmur, keeping it intentionally vague. I did say only one question, after all.

"Ooh, like in a kinky way?"

I muffle a laugh. "No, Aub. Get your head out of the gutter. We just had to play things sort of safe."

As if there's anything even remotely safe about hooking up in a house full of his entire extended family. What we did last night was the sexual equivalent of lighting a match next to a gas pump. Dangerous, if not a little stupid. But, *damn*, the heat was worth it.

After a few more minutes of talking galas and guys, I hear the creak of the front door paired with the crinkling of paper bags. Lolli and Tess must be back with party decorations.

"I should probably go. There's a party for Asher's grandma tomorrow that I think we're going to start decorating for."

"All right. I guess I should go grab lunch before I'm lost in spreadsheet hell again," Aubree says, sounding bored. "But if anything else goes down, literally or figuratively, I'd better be getting a call about it the second it happens." She pauses for a moment, then adds, "Well, maybe not the second it happens. Probably after you, like, get your clothes back on and leave the room. But I'd better be the first to know."

"Pinkie swear." I stick my pinkie up in the air, despite the fact that my best friend isn't here to link her own little finger with it.

"I'm actually holding my pinkie out right now," Aubree says. "Is that lame or just a sign that I'm serious about this?"

"A little bit of both, I think," I say with a grin. "But I'm doing it too."

Aubree laughs. "Okay, I'm going to grab something to eat. Go and get your man, and by *get your man*, I mean get his dick."

CHAPTER ELEVEN

Living My Best Life

Asher

My cousins Mack and Tyson talked me into surfing today, even though I'm not sure it's the best idea, given that I'm still injured. But they're a couple of years older than me, and I've always fallen headfirst into their peer pressure. It's the reason why I tried my first (and last) cigarette at age thirteen. It's why I climbed a water tower at their dare at seventeen, and sprained my wrist on the way down.

And now it's the reason why I'm standing in the surf, wearing boardshorts with a surfboard lying on the sand next to me, even though it's the last thing I want to be doing right now. What I'd rather be doing is finding Bailey, but she's off doing something with Amber this morning, and I've yet to talk to her since last night.

We hung out a little bit yesterday after that amazing hookup in my room, but it was with my entire family, so it wasn't exactly conducive to finding out how she might be feeling. And then she excused herself early, just after nine, saying she was tired, and headed up to bed. Alone.

Trust me, if I could have sneaked away to join her, I would have. But Fable challenged me to a game of Uno, and I wasn't about to crush a six-year-old by skipping out. Plus, hello there, competitive streak. I won two hands, and Fable beat me once.

Maybe that epic orgasm tired Bailey out. It's a nice thought, and one I would have liked to have held on to, but when I finally went up to bed around eleven, I noticed her light was still on. I didn't know what to make of that, so I just went to bed, but it took me a while to fall asleep.

"Hey, come on, man!" Mack calls, motioning for me to join him in the water. He's about waist deep, and his board bobs beside him in the swells. The water is warm enough this time of year that no one's wearing a wet suit.

Tyson, the more adventurous and daring of the two, doesn't wait for anyone, and he's already stretched out on his board, paddling toward the breakers.

God fucking dammit. Where is Bailey to talk me out of this?

I grab my board and splash into the water, hoping like hell I don't hurt myself. With how distracted I am today, it'll be a wonder if I can even stand up.

When I finally paddle out to where Tyson and Mack wait for me, I'm out of breath and they're both grinning.

"You made it, precious. Are you actually winded, dude?" Tyson asks, a cocky grin plastered on his face.

I'd like to see them join me on the ice. We'd see who gets winded pretty damn fast.

Last time I was on water that wasn't frozen was ages ago. I haven't surfed since I was a kid. Thankfully, the water is warm and the sun is shining, and it helps lift my mood. I ride a couple of easy waves, but for the most part, I'm content just sitting on my board, watching my cousins make fools of themselves competing against each other.

When Tyson takes off on a wave, Mack looks over at me. "So, what's the story with Bailey? Is she single?"

I open my mouth to tell him to back off, but the words get caught in my throat. Because Bailey is single, even if I don't necessarily want her to be.

Before I can even respond, he says under his breath, "Well, speak of the devil." I follow his gaze to the shore where Bailey has ventured down onto the sand, carrying a beach towel and a paperback.

She gives us a wave, then plops herself down on the towel and begins reading her book. For her sake, I hope it's not a medical text. She works too hard, and this week is supposed to be relaxing for her.

"Good wave coming," Mack says, glancing behind us at the swell that's gaining speed.

"You hit it. I'm going in to talk to Bailey." Lying down on the board, I let the water push me in to the shore, and climb off the board when I reach the sand.

Bailey watches me, shielding her eyes from the sun. "I'm not sure that surfing was on Trey's list of approved activities, sir," she says when I get closer. "But I guess I should have realized you'd be a rule breaker."

I laugh. "I promise what I did could barely be described as surfing. I'm sure you'll hear all about what a pussy I was when Mack and Ty come in."

She shakes her head. "Then I won't listen to a word of it so your street cred stays intact."

I'm pleased to see her book isn't a textbook, but instead is the crime thriller I saw her looking at in the airport. "Is your book any good?"

She frowns down at it for a second before meeting my eyes. "I wouldn't actually know. I haven't made it past page two."

I don't ask her why, but a small part of me hopes it's because the sight of me in board shorts is as distracting to her as she is to me.

Gorgeous, pale creamy curves fill out her two-piece suit so perfectly, I have to grip my surfboard hard enough to bruise my palms so I don't reach out and touch her. But the truth is, she's so much more than a hot girl . . . she's fun and smart and sweet. I like our conversations. I like just being near her, period.

When I sit down next to her in the sand and ask about her visit to the hospital yesterday, she tells me all about her outing with my sisters, and about how Nora loved her slippers and eagerly tore into the trail mix. And about how the normally composed Amber cried when she held the baby for the first time. While we talk, we watch Mack and Tyson catch wave after wave. Both of them showing off for Bailey's benefit, that much is obvious, at least to me.

Wanting to take her eyes off of them and bring them back to me, I ask, "So, are you glad you came?"

Her answering smile tells me everything I need to know. "Without a doubt."

A few minutes later, I hear the sound of Lolli's voice calling us from the house. "I'm going to head back up and see what she needs. Are you going to stay down here?"

Bailey hops up and dusts sand from her legs. "No, I think I'll come with you."

Something inside me is pleased that she doesn't care about watching the show my cousins are putting on. She'd rather be with me.

• • •

"I think that's the last of it." I set the case of wine

down on the counter and use the bottom of my T-shirt to wipe the sweat from my forehead. Bailey and I spent the last hour running a few errands for my mom, which included picking up more wine for the party.

"Thanks, honey," Mom says, grabbing the bottles two at a time to stick in the fridge.

"Anything else I can help you with, Tess?" Bailey asks.

Mom shakes her head. "No. Go relax. Thank you, though."

Bailey grabs a bottle of water from the fridge and hands a second one to me. I down it in one go.

"Any news on Nora and the baby?" Bailey asks my mom as she takes a sip of her own water.

"They're going to release her in time for the birthday bash tomorrow. I think she sweet-talked the nurses, but the baby's healthy, so it's all fine."

"Oh, that's great news." Bailey smiles.

Tossing my water bottle into the recycling bin, I press a kiss to my mom's cheek. "I'm going to go shower."

Bailey nods, watching me. She's quiet, and I

have no idea what's on her mind. But a few minutes after I climb the stairs and strip off my T-shirt, Bailey slips into my bedroom, closing the door behind her.

"Hey," I say, turning to face her.

"I thought I'd see if you could use a hand."

"Showering?" I ask hopefully, my lower half starting to throb.

Bailey nods and crosses the room toward me.

I choke on a laugh when I realize, *oh fuck,* she's serious. A hot shudder rocks through me as I watch her approach. I love how forward she is. Love how sex-positive and open she is. It's like she just fits me and my personality. I've always been an *if it feels good, do it* kind of guy, and it seems like that's exactly what Bailey's thinking too.

She stops right in front of me like we're playing a game of chicken. Someone needs to tap out. Otherwise, I can't be held responsible for all the wicked things I want to do to her.

With my fingers under her chin, I lift her mouth to mine, which isn't exactly a smooth move because our height difference is such that I have to sort of bend my knees and hunch over. But the second her mouth presses against mine, I stop giving a fuck and just go with it, because *holy shit*, Bailey is a good kisser.

It's deep and messy, and her tongue matches mine stroke for stroke. My heart rate builds and my fingers sink into her hair as her mouth stays fused to mine in the hottest kiss I've had in a long time. Maybe in forever.

"I like kissing you way too much," she murmurs against my lips.

Same, sweetheart. "It's a good problem to have, I guess."

I press one more sweet kiss to her mouth, but I straighten when I feel her fingers working at the button on my shorts. My cock perks up immediately.

"You sure?" I ask, lifting her chin so I can meet her eyes. They're bright and clear, and determined.

"You assured me all systems were in perfect working order," she teases.

"And what . . . you want to see for yourself?" I can't help but smile.

"Something like that." She bites her lip as she frees the button to my shorts and then slowly draws down the zipper.

All the breath leaves my lungs at once the second her warm palm slides inside my boxer briefs.

Fuck.

I push both hands through my hair, dropping my head back to stare straight up at the ceiling. Well, not really staring. My eyes are squeezed tight because I can't freaking believe that Bailey is the woman sliding her hand up and down over me. It feels so freaking amazing.

"Jeez, Ashe," she says on a gasp, drawing my length from my shorts and giving me an appreciative look.

I'm not gonna lie; my chest puffs out a little with pride. But then I can't focus on anything else, because Bailey knows exactly how to handle my favorite appendage. Long, firm strokes that make my abdominal muscles tighten.

"Fuck. That feels good," I whisper, finding her mouth with mine again.

As I thrust into her fist, a shiver rolls through me. I groan, unable to do anything but make rough, inarticulate sounds that vibrate through the small bathroom.

"How set are you on this shower?" I glance at the tiny shower stall, and then at the big bed in the other room.

"I don't mind you a little sweaty." The grin on her full mouth is cheeky and playful.

I did shower this morning after surfing. How gross could I have gotten running errands for an hour?

But when Bailey lowers herself to her knees in front of me and looks up at me with her big brown eyes, the decision is made for me.

CHAPTER TWELVE

Expect the Unexpected

Bailey

I'm a smart girl who's capable of many things, but practicing restraint around Asher Reed isn't one of them.

When I drop to my knees on the bathroom floor right in front of him, his lips part on a shaky breath, which quickly becomes a stuttered moan when I wrap my hand around him. To answer Aubree's question, Asher doesn't disappoint in the endowment department. There's a lot of him, and I'm eager to please every solid inch.

From the moment I saw him on the beach this morning, his blond hair wet and tousled with sea water, biceps flexing as he lugged that surfboard up the shoreline, I knew what I wanted. Him. Like this. Stripped down and fully at my disposal. And just a few short hours later, that's exactly what I have, and I don't even know where to start. I'm greedy, and Asher offers so much.

He stands over me like a statue carved from granite—utterly still except for his sculpted chest, which hitches with short, uneven breaths, as his thick length throbs in my hands.

I run my palm from his base to his swollen tip, testing his size with lazy, teasing strokes. I know I should take things slow and enjoy every inch and moment, exactly like he did with me last night. But it's hard to go slow with him gazing down at me with a desperate, yet appreciative expression.

"Oh fuck," he whispers as I welcome the first few inches of him into my mouth. A low, satisfied hum rumbles in his chest. *This man. God.* This huge, hulking, muscular beast of a man is coming apart, and it's all for me.

I wish I could bottle the noises he's making. Deep groans, halting breaths, and the most delicious-sounding choked grunts. But I can't do that, of course. I can't even focus long enough on those sexy noises to confidently commit them to memory because I'm too lost in the moment, too far gone. Too drunk on him and all this brooding, sexual masculinity to even focus on gathering breath in my lungs. I suck in a shocked gasp of air and bring my mouth to him again, treating the broad tip of him to a slow, wet kiss.

You know when you're really bringing your A game—and, trust me, this is my A+ game. Wet from my curious mouth, his length slides deep easily and I swallow him down, my hands pumping his base while my mouth does wicked things that make his abs tighten and his thighs tremble.

"Jesus, Bailey." He swallows the words. "Gonna fucking kill me."

The muscles in his thighs bunch as I start to bob my head, and I can tell we're both hanging on to the last threads of our self-control. All it takes is one more taste of him, and the threads snap. I can't tease him for another second.

Hold on tight, Ashe. I'm going to take you for the ride of a lifetime.

"Yes, just like that." He fights off a hard shiver as his hand slips into the hair at the back of my neck. Not tugging on it, or urging me closer, just enjoying the feel of us joining together this way. I like it way too much.

I can't resist peeking up at him to see if his expression matches the delicious, sexy noises he's making. As I look up at him through my lashes, my hands and mouth still steadily working him over, our gazes meet just long enough for me to lose myself in the sapphire of his eyes. They're the deep blue of a stormy sea, and just one glance has me drowning in them, shipwrecked with no hope of survival. At least, that's what it feels like in this moment.

And then those perfect, stormy blue eyes sink closed. He bites his bottom lip, a desperate attempt to hold back the groan building in his chest. But even through his clenched teeth, I can hear his need, can feel it vibrating through him. I know the feeling all too well—it's the same one pulsating between my thighs. But just as I feel his body stiffen and his muscles jump, he pulls away.

"Is . . . is something wrong?" I ask, panting with need. Maybe I wasn't doing as good of a job as I thought, but I could have sworn I had him right on the edge. "Don't you want to, you know, finish?"

"I was about to," he says, looking down at me with kind eyes. "But I need to get you there first."

A hot chill races through me. That is by far the sexiest thing a man has ever said to me. And as much as I want to take him up on the offer, I'd be stupid not to consider his injury first. "What about your leg?"

"My leg will be fine. You've taken good care of it." A smirk tugs at the corner of his lips. "You've taken damn good care of my third leg too. But no way am I finishing without getting you off too."

He helps me to my feet, pulling me in for a deep, grateful kiss. "Bedroom," he growls against my mouth.

I don't know if it's a suggestion, a request, or a command. However he intended it, I'm perched on the edge of his bed in a matter of seconds, shimmying my denim shorts down to the floor. When Asher spots the pink swimsuit bottoms I have on underneath, he shakes his head in disbelief.

"That damn pink bikini." He sighs. "I think that thing is my weakness."

"Maybe I should wear it more often then."

"You should." A wicked flicker dances through his eyes as he loops his thumbs into the waistband. "But right now, I need it gone."

A shudder rolls through me as he tugs the hot-pink nylon to the floor. Next goes my T-shirt, and finally, with a pull of the bow holding up my bikini top, there's not a trace of clothing between the two of us. Nothing but skin on skin, kissing and rubbing and heat more searing than the sun. I lean back against the pillows, and Asher takes his time, exploring every inch of my curves with his calloused fingers.

"Good Lord, Bailey." He cups my breasts in his hands, sweeping his tongue over his bottom lip as he thumbs my nipples. "These are fucking perfect."

My breathing grows ragged, and I try to push my lower half toward his. I guide one of his hands to the space between my legs, letting him know what I want, and he groans in approval.

"Fucking incredible," he whispers. "So wet. So perfect."

And then, for the second time this evening, Asher pulls back. He gets up from the bed and digs into his duffel, fishing out a silver wrapper.

"Just in case," he says, meeting my eyes.

A hot thrill runs through me at his low, sultry words. In case I want to have sex. Why does he think that would even be a question? Doesn't he know how hot he is? How much I want him? Even if the next few days are all I get….

"You packed condoms?" I ask with a grin,

propping myself up on my elbows to get a good view of his sexy physique as he moves back onto the bed beside me. "Were you expecting something between you and me?"

"Of course not. This was entirely unexpected." He kneels between my parted thighs and runs one warm palm over my calf muscle. "Hoped for? Sure. But not expected." He presses a sweet, gentle kiss against my eager mouth, tugging lightly on my bottom lip with his teeth as he pulls back. "You okay?"

The look in his blue gaze is sincere, and I realize I feel the exact same way. I never expected this, but I did secretly hope we'd end up here.

Then he nods toward the condom lying beside us on the bed. "Should I put that on?"

"God, yes," I say, a half sigh, half plea. I've been ready for this since the night I had too many of Lolli's cocktails and followed him up to his room. It may have only been a few days ago, but it's felt like half a lifetime of waiting.

Before I can think twice, Asher has suited up and is back to his spot between my parted thighs, rocking his hips into mine. I gather a breath into my lungs as he sinks into me, delicious slow inch by delicious slow inch. And, *good God*, he was worth the wait.

"F-fuck, Ashe," I stutter, my hips rising to meet his, eager for every inch.

"Hmm," he groans, simultaneously posing no question in particular and a hundred questions all at once. But words aren't necessary. I know exactly what he's asking.

Is that good?

Should I keep going?

Can I go deeper?

Can I make you come this way?

I answer all of the unspoken questions at once on a desperate sigh. "Yes."

He presses his lips to mine, quieting me as he moves, leaving me breathless and digging my fingernails into his back. Even when he breaks our kiss, his lips hover over mine as our hips move in time together. We're breathing the same air, moving to the same rhythm, crashing into each other like tides against the shore. It's not good, it's not even great—it's mind blowing.

When he brings one hand to my clit, drawing

circles around it with his thumb, I lose all hope of hanging on any longer. Soon I'm clenching against his length, right on the edge of my orgasm.

"Holy fuck, Asher." I gasp. "I'm going to—"

"Me too, baby."

With a few final thrusts, we go tumbling over the edge together, one after the other. I don't even know who goes first. But we're together in this moment, him and me, grinding our hips and riding out the last of our own separate storms.

Keep your day on the beach. This, right here, is freaking paradise.

As I come down from my high, I don't get to float back to reality as I would have hoped. Instead, I'm shot out of the sky as the look of bliss on Asher's face morphs from an appreciative smile to a slight frown, then turns into a full-on grimace.

"Fucking shit."

"What's wrong? Are you okay?" Panic rises in my throat as he eases out of me and rolls onto his side, gripping his thigh.

Of course he's not okay. He's recovering from a serious injury and was specifically instructed to avoid vigorous activity. And what we just did definitely qualifies as vigorous. Holy shit, how am I going to explain this to Trey?

"I'm fine." He hisses out the words through clenched teeth. Tentatively, he drags one hand along his inner thigh, and his face twists again as he sucks in a sharp breath. "But my leg might not be."

I clap one hand over my mouth, leaping to my feet. "Oh my God, Ashe, I'm so sorry. Do you need ice? Do you need an Advil?" I fumble for my bikini and my denim cutoffs, getting dressed faster than a high schooler after gym class.

It's official, I'm the worst doctor ever. I'd better start drafting an apology note to Trey and start reconsidering careers.

Asher smiles, sitting up in bed and combing his fingers through his tousled blond locks. "Please don't freak out. Every moment of that was totally worth it."

I raise a brow at him. "Really? Is sex with me really worth sustaining a secondary injury?"

He doesn't miss a beat. "Yes. And I'd do it again in a heartbeat." He rubs his swollen inner thigh, flinching at the soreness. "But you're right. I should probably ice this."

I let out a shaky exhale as I retrieve his shorts, making sure he's decent before I open the door to go retrieve an ice pack from the freezer. On my way, I pass by Lolli and Tess, who are busy arranging centerpieces for tomorrow's party, but they just wave as I pass. They don't suspect a thing. My trips to the freezer for Asher's ice packs have been a routine part of the week. For all they know, this time is no different. They might find out about his aggravated injury, but no way am I letting them find out what caused it.

When I return to his room, Asher has taken care of the condom and gotten dressed. When I sit down beside him on the bed, he smiles up at me, scooting closer. He knows the drill by now, hiking up the leg of his shorts so I can ice the most swollen part of his thigh. When I press the ice pack against his leg, he cringes a bit more than usual, but a precursory glance at the swelling doesn't indicate any additional damage.

"What's the verdict, Doc?" he asks after I've inspected him for a moment.

"I think we've got one very aggravated groin sprain, and one very guilty-feeling doctor."

He laughs, giving me a soft look. "Don't feel guilty. I'm the one who suggested we take this to bed. It takes two to tango, you know."

I weigh his words, drawing a slow breath. "That's true. And the good news is, if we'd taken you from a grade-two to a grade-three pulled muscle, you'd probably be screaming right now. So the fact that you're doing well enough to get up and get dressed suggests that we may have only set you back a few days of recovery."

"I can handle that." He shrugs.

"Let me know if you notice any additional bruising. We need you in good shape so you can soon be out there on the ice with your team again," I say, squeezing his shoulder. "Need anything else?"

He looks up at me with a hope-filled expression. "A kiss good night?"

I smile, tracing the angle of his jaw with my fingertips. "To use your words, I can handle that."

CHAPTER THIRTEEN

Celebrations

Asher

"**W**hat in the world?" Lolli frowns at me as I hobble past her, limping on my way to the coffee maker. "Rough night, sugarplum?"

Fuck. I can't exactly tell my grandmother that the gorgeous houseguest she opened her home to re-sprained my groin when I rode her too hard last night. Even if it was totally worth it, and I'd do it a hundred times over.

"No. I'm fine," I lie. Wincing silently, I grip the countertop hard enough to turn my knuckles white.

"Fine, my tail feather. Go sit down. I'll bring you coffee. And some frozen peas." Lolli waves me from the room and I shuffle into the sunroom, sinking onto the rattan sofa carefully.

Ouch.

Less than a minute later, she's back, standing before me with that same worried expression. "Here you go." Lolli sets a steaming mug of coffee on the table in front of me and hands me the same bag of frozen peas I used my first day here.

"Oh. Almost forgot . . . Happy birthday, Lolli." I look up at her and grin.

"Thanks, honey. It's so nice to have the family all together to celebrate."

I nod. The big party is tonight.

I can't believe how fast this week has gone by. I also can't believe how wrapped up in Bailey I've been. But one thing's for certain—I regret nothing.

Lolli's mouth lifts in a conspiratorial grin as she watches me. "I went by Bailey's room last night to see if she wanted to join me for tea on the veranda this morning, but she wasn't in her bedroom."

"I wouldn't know anything about that." I take a casual sip of my coffee.

"You were always a terrible liar, Ashe."

I grin at her. "Have a good day, Lolli."

With a chuckle, Lolli wanders back into the

kitchen.

Later that day, Nora and Todd are released from the hospital with my brand-new niece, Hannah. She's so tiny and pink and adorable. And since neither of us can do more than lounge around, I end up holding her most of the day while I'm camped out on the couch. Nora and Todd take turns napping, and Nora stops by every two hours to nurse Hannah, but for the most part, the baby and I are left to our own devices. Me, sprawled across the sofa with ice and tape on my leg, and Hannah wrapped neatly like a burrito, resting on my chest.

The hockey game is on in the background, but I can hardly bring myself to watch it. My team is down by two games this series, and I feel sick that I'm not there to help them. I've never been more thankful for all the distractions of the big family reunion that's about to get underway.

My cousins are helping set up extra outdoor tables and chairs, and Bailey is helping my mom in the kitchen. She threatened anyone who asked if I was able to help, and has made sure I've been off my feet all day, which I'm pretty thankful for.

When Nora comes to nurse Hannah again, I decide it's time to get myself ready for this party. With a groan, I slowly make it up the stairs and shower.

As I emerge from my room dressed in jeans and a T-shirt, Bailey is just leaving her room too. She stops in front of me, dressed in a light blue cotton dress with buttons down the front. Her feet are bare, which means she looks even tinier, and dangling from her hand are a pair of sandals.

"Hey." I grin down at her.

"Hey, yourself. How are you feeling?"

Ignoring her question, I softly touch her cheek. "I want you in my bed tonight."

Bailey's lips part on an inhale. "I don't want to injure you again."

"That was totally worth it," I say in earnest, but Bailey gives me an uncertain look. "You ready for this party?" I grin, trying to lighten the mood.

"I can't say I've ever been to an eighty-fifth birthday party before." She chuckles, her cheeks turning the softest shade of pink.

I smile back at her. I would have been happy to stand here lost in the warmth of her eyes, but the noise from the party carries up the stairs, pulling Bailey's attention away. The shock of hearty laughter from Lolli is a welcome sound, though.

I've been becoming all too aware of the need to commit that sound to memory. Aware of the fact that my funny, loving, and sometimes intrusive grandmother isn't going to be around forever.

But before I can dwell on it further, Bailey flashes me a kind smile and starts down the stairs. I quickly follow.

The party is already in full swing. A three-piece jazz band is setting up on the back deck. The kitchen counters hold aluminum chafing trays covered in foil, and the aroma of Mexican food from Miguel's—my favorite restaurant on the island—makes me grateful I resisted a second helping at lunch. Because I'm going to crush whatever is in those trays.

Various wines and bottles of local beer are chilling in ice buckets, and several pitchers of Lolli's very potent special juice have been prepared. My mom took care not to mix them too strong, but I wouldn't be surprised if Lolli sneaked in behind her and spiked them. A platter of cheese has been artfully arranged on the kitchen island with little edible flowers and bunches of grapes providing pops of color. Later, there will be a bonfire on the beach and dancing.

No detail was overlooked, and no expense has

been spared. I made sure of that.

Mom handled all the planning, with Lolli providing opinions and direction, and I provided the credit card number. Lolli was firm in only one thing—that our presence here is the only gift she wants. And I sure hope she was serious about that, because despite my reservations about showing up empty-handed, that's exactly what I've done.

"Fudgesicles," Bailey says, pausing at the bottom of the stairs. My family's habit of made-up curse words has apparently rubbed off on her already. "I didn't even think of it until now, but I didn't get Lolli a gift."

I shake my head. "She requested no gifts. Our being here is enough. That's all she wants."

Bailey frowns and waves one hand. "That's just something women say. We don't actually mean it."

Shit.

"Is that true?" Mack asks, appearing out of nowhere from behind us.

Lolli stops beside Bailey and gives us a wink. "It's normally true."

Bailey chuckles, and Mack and I exchange a confused look.

Wait, what?

"But this time, it's totally legit," Lolli says, sounding decades younger. "There's not a single thing from a store shelf that would have made me happier than having all of you here celebrating my birthday."

Bailey smiles, looping her arm through Lolli's. "I think the birthday girl needs a special birthday cocktail."

With a chuckle, Lolli accompanies Bailey to the kitchen, while I wander over to check on Nora and the baby.

Over the course of the evening, I stuff myself with tamales, flank steak, green-chili enchiladas, and enough queso to feed a small village. I chat with my mom and sisters. I dance with Lolli until Fable cuts in, and then I dance with her until Tad says it's past her bedtime. All the while feeling Bailey's eyes on me.

Wondering what may happen later between Bailey and me is totally normal, right? Because the sex? It was totally hot. On a scale of one to *I'm ready to get down on one knee and propose* hot—let's just say I'm marching through some uncharted territory.

Does it scare me? A little, but I'm more concerned with how I can convince her to come to bed with me again. Although I realize in that moment that's not quite right. Bailey was the one who propositioned me that first night. She let herself into my room with the intention of riding me like a bull at the rodeo. And I was so down with that scenario.

As the evening passes, I'm happy to see Lolli's smile has remained firmly in place. When it's time for cake, though, she begins to look a little weepy. A thousand candles sparkle on top of the three-tiered confection with yellow frosting and pink flamingos piped in hot-pink icing. We sing horribly loud, and off-key while Lolli wipes her eyes with a handkerchief made from one of Pop's old flannel shirts.

Damn, I'll admit I'm having a hard time keeping my own eyes dry. Bailey stands next to me the entire time, squeezing my hand. I'm not going to lie that my brain doesn't start spinning ideas about someday having a love as deep as Lolli and Pops'.

Over a slice of cake, I make a point to sit and talk with my dad for a while, since I don't get to do that nearly enough. He asks a lot of questions about the team, and I enjoy talking hockey with him, even if I am bitterly pissed that I can't play right now.

A little while later, guests begin to filter out and retire to bed. When the party has died down and the band has packed up following their three-hour set, and most of the family has gone, I sit on the back deck with my mom, enjoying my first adult beverage of the evening. I haven't had any dizziness or headaches for several days now, so I'm confident that the concussion isn't a concern any longer. Bailey waves good-night to everyone and gives Lolli a big hug, then goes on up to bed.

The grown-up inside me plays it cool, when all I want to do is sprint up the stairs after her and attack her mouth with kisses. Instead, I remain seated where I am, forcing my gaze down into my glass of bourbon.

"So," Mom says once it's just us again. "You and Bailey?"

"Nah." I rub the back of my neck with one hand, really not wanting to have this conversation with my mom when I don't even know what the hell is going on. "I don't think so."

Her eyes soften. "Well, you'll never know unless you try. I've never known you as someone who doesn't chase what he wants. If Bailey is the woman you want in your life, then chase her with as much passion and determination as you did to get the hockey career you currently have."

I focus on my glass of bourbon and don't say anything else. Mom's right. When I want something, I don't stop until it's mine. Whether it's playing for my favorite team, getting the position I want, buying the perfect apartment in the best part of Seattle. What I want, I've always gotten because I never gave up.

And I want Bailey. I can't and won't deny that.

But she made it pretty fucking clear that she doesn't want a relationship. My job takes me on the road for more time than I'll be home in Seattle. Her career is going to keep her ridiculously busy. On paper, we would never work. I know that. But I still want her. Desperately. Even if I'm not ready to admit that.

"It's not that simple," I say, keeping my tone neutral.

Mom releases a long sigh, still staring straight ahead. "I don't want your father's and my marriage impeding your decisions. We were young, and..."

I hold up one hand, stopping her. "Mom, there's no need to feel guilty. I know you and dad are happier apart. I've made peace with that. Seriously, there's no need to trudge up the past."

She hums, giving me a thoughtful look. "Okay. I'd just love to see you with a good girl at some point, Asher."

"I know, Mom. Me too."

"Someone you can bring home to the family. Someone like Bailey," she adds.

I press my lips together.

Mom's soft voice interrupts my thoughts as she stands up and places her hand on my shoulder. "I like her, Asher. I really like her. For our family, and most of all for you. If you want her, don't let her go."

I watch Mom disappear inside as I finish the rest of my bourbon. But it's not the strong liquor that swims through my mind, it's the thought of the gorgeous girl upstairs.

CHAPTER FOURTEEN

Bye-Bye, Certainty

Bailey

Seven days ago, I couldn't have imagined the feelings currently stirring inside me. And I have one very hot hockey player to blame.

Prior to this trip, my life was simple. Orderly. Everything made sense.

I worked, I studied, I worked some more. I occasionally slept, and complained to my girlfriends about how single I was—but I knew what I wanted. And that was to focus on myself and my career. I've never needed a man, never need someone to complete me. I loved being an independent woman. It was part of my identity. Now, things are slightly cloudier.

Am I still super excited about going home to start my residency? Of course. But the part where

I go back to being just friends with Asher? That's a little less clear in my head.

How do you go back to being just friends with a man you've heard gasp out your name in a lustful groan? A man who is so sexy your stomach literally erupts with butterflies from a simple smile?

It's like I can't stop looking at him differently now—this golden boy with his perfectly chiseled abs and his bright, playful eyes and his honey-colored hair. Now that I've witnessed his softer side, as well as knowing his rough-and-tumble hockey/ playboy persona he lives by back home—well, it's changed a few things.

His warmth and affection for his family, even its littlest members, is so endearing. When I watched him working at opening a bottle of cranberry juice for his grandmother earlier, it stirred something deep inside me. Which is why I excused myself, said my good-nights, and rushed up to bed. It was either go up to bed, or else ravish him in front of his family. Even though I assume Lolli would be okay with that, it definitely isn't how I want her birthday to be remembered.

After brushing my teeth and changing into sleep shorts and a tank top, I crawl between the sheets. But sleep doesn't come easily . . . and neither does the ability to turn off my thoughts of Asher.

I loved just looking at him tonight. The clench of his chiseled jaw as he reacted to something Mack had said. The casual way he rested his bulky arm across one of my shoulders. The easy way his mouth lifted in a smile when Fable darted past. The love that sparkle in his eyes when he looked at his baby niece, Hannah. Not to mention that I can't seem to forget the way he kisses—a kiss so firm and insistent and hot that my toes curl against the sheets even now.

And then I have a terrible thought. A girl could fall in love with Asher very easily. Too easily.

I have no idea what to do with that information, other than push it away faster than a hockey player can slap a puck into a net.

CHAPTER FIFTEEN

Mixed Bag

Asher

After the party is over and the mess in the kitchen is cleaned up, I trudge up the stairs and let out a defeated sigh when I see that Bailey's door is closed and there's no light coming from beneath her door. I guess I have my answer.

I'll be sleeping alone tonight.

Maybe it's for the best. My groin still throbs, and I don't particularly want to reinjure it. Of course, I wouldn't say no if Bailey decided to join me later.

I slip into my room without bothering to turn on the light. After using the bathroom, I brush my teeth and then shuck off my shorts and T-shirt, then crawl into bed.

The memory of what Bailey and I shared in this bed slams into me, and arousal thrums low, heat stirring in my veins. I'm just considering jerking off when a warm body rolls over next to me, settling close.

"Bailey?" I say with surprise.

"Ashe," she murmurs, rolling closer and placing one palm flat against my abs.

My body responds immediately, my cock hardening at the first sound of her husky, sleep-laced voice.

"What are you . . ."

The rest of that sentence goes unspoken because warm lips press against mine in a sleepy kiss. I don't get the chance to ask her what she's doing here, but she makes it obvious, kissing me eagerly.

Rolling to my side until our bodies are flush, I fit my mouth over hers and deepen the kiss. Bailey's lips part, welcoming my tongue, and I groan deeply.

But it still isn't enough, so I push up onto my elbows, moving on top of her until I can cage her in with my forearms and press my throbbing erection right between her thighs. Bailey lets out a satisfied sound, somewhere between a sigh and a moan. I'm on the exact same page. It's both a relief—easing the ache just a fraction—but not remotely enough to satisfy.

But then Bailey does the most brilliant thing. She opens her thighs wider until I can fit the head of my cock right against her warm center, where I rub and grind and tease as her tongue flirts with mine.

"Oh fuck, Ashe," she whispers, her voice sounding breathy and desperate. "I want your cock."

"Yes, sweetheart. It's yours." Now. Tonight. Next week. Forever.

That last thought should scare the shit out of me, but it doesn't. Not even a little.

Before I can plot my next move, Bailey's hands are between us, working into my boxer briefs, pushing them down over my ass until her hot palm is working up and down over my straining cock.

Fuck.

It feels so damn good. A shudder races through me, and I let out a groan that Bailey drinks down. Holding my weight above her with one arm, I bring my other hand between us, pushing my fingers into the side of her underwear to rub her warm, wet heat.

"We'll be careful this time," she says on a gasp.

"So careful," I murmur.

Thrusting her hips up into mine, Bailey takes control, coating me in her wetness, and trying to work my dick inside.

My relief is instantaneous. I like her in charge, and groan my appreciation. "Yes, sweetheart."

Bailey squirms, closing the gap between us until the head of my cock wedges just inside her snug pussy. It feels incredible, and her answering moan is the best sound in the world.

Then realization slams into me like a freight train.

"Condom," I croak, my voice hoarse.

"Right," she answers, dislodging the best feeling I've ever had.

I move off her, but only long enough to retrieve a condom and suit up. Once I'm secure, I lie flat on the bed and pull Bailey on top of me.

"Ride me," I say on a groan when she rocks against me teasingly.

Barely a second later, Bailey is lifting herself up on her knees and finding the right angle to join us. She slides down slowly, allowing us both to adjust to the overwhelming sensations. It's like being punched in the face—with pleasure, instead of pain. It's way too much, and it's fucking perfect.

Bailey trembles on top of me as she slides all the way down until I'm fully buried in the tightest heat I've ever felt. I let out a monstrous groan as hot arousal flickers wildly through my veins.

I place my hand on her hip to guide her, but Bailey doesn't need any direction. She rolls her hips like she's been training for this moment for years, rather than studying for a medical degree. Honest to God, if you told me she was a dick-riding champion instead of a medical student, in this moment, I would have believed you.

Working together, kissing often, we race toward our release. When Bailey brings one hand between us to touch herself, I brush it away.

"My job, sweetheart."

Her answering groan is audible. "Yes, yes, yes. I'm so close."

And I'll get her there—that's no question. But I'm still learning her body, still figuring out that slow, deep thrusts make her breath catch in her throat and her fingernails curl into my biceps. Tiny helpless whimpers fall from her perfect lips as my fingers continue moving between us.

Then I feel it—the delicious squeeze of her body around mine. She leans over me, falling onto my chest. She nuzzles my throat, her lips scraping the stubble on my jaw.

"Ashe," she says on a low moan as her orgasm pulses between us, seeming to go on forever.

I rock into her, pressing deeper, and the feeling of her tight heat squeezing me propels me over the edge. "Fuck, Bailey. It's too good."

Cupping one hand against her jaw, I tilt her chin, fitting my mouth across hers. At the first hot sweep of her eager tongue against mine, I lose the last of my self-control. Thrusting into her in short, uneven strokes, my entire body goes rigid, ready to explode. Bailey murmurs encouraging things into my ear as I empty myself into the condom in hot, pulsing waves. I feel light-headed when it's over.

Holy hell.

The intensity of what we just shared deserves to be acknowledged. But rather than talk, or cuddle, or even just lie together while we catch our breath,

Bailey climbs from the bed and begins hunting for her clothes.

"You can stay," I say, sitting up to watch her pull on her underwear.

"That's okay." She grabs her tank top. "I'm sure you'll sleep better without me in your space."

I doubt that's true, but her dismissal of this moment between us leaves me momentarily speechless. My mood sinks faster than a slap shot into an empty net.

What the hell is happening?

"Your leg okay?" she asks, glancing toward me.

I nod absently. My leg is the last thing on my mind right now.

A second later, Bailey presses a quick kiss to my mouth, and then leaves me there alone still wearing a damp condom.

For as much heat had filled this room just moments ago, it now feels cold and empty.

CHAPTER SIXTEEN

Catch Flights, Not Feelings

Bailey

"**U***gh*. Close, you bastard," I groan under my breath.

I feel like my suitcase is an impossible game of Tetris. Move a pair of shoes. Rotate my makeup bag. Try putting my shampoo in vertical instead of horizontal.

I've been sitting on my bedroom floor packing for the last half hour, but no amount of rearranging, squishing, or pleading with my belongings has made everything fit. I've even switched outfits, trading in my T-shirt for a more structured top that was taking up more space. No luck.

After resituating a pair of sandals for what has to be the tenth time, I put all the muscle I have into giving the zipper another tug. *Nope*. It still doesn't budge.

Why is it that everything always fits in my suitcase when I'm packing for a trip, but on the way back, it's like my stuff has multiplied by ten? Add it to the list of things I will never understand. Along with black holes, the male metabolism, and, most recently, my feelings for Asher.

I've had such an incredible time with him this week, both in and out of the bedroom. But this week was vacation, not real life. And in real life, I'm way too busy to make time for a relationship. My life is kind of like this suitcase—so filled to the brim that if I try to add one more thing, it just won't fit.

Let's be honest, it's not like Asher is relationship material anyway.

"Need a hand?"

Asher appears in my doorway, his duffel bag slung over one shoulder. He's wearing joggers and his Ice Hawks hat turned backward. His eyes are bright, and he looks like this week recharged him some.

My emotions are tangled and a little bittersweet, because it feels like something is coming to an end. I wish we could go back to then, back to when we had a whole week of sun and sexual tension ahead of us.

"I need more than a hand." I sigh, giving the zipper another useless tug. "I need a trash compactor."

He chuckles, setting his duffel down and crouching to my level. "You sit on it, and I'll pull the zipper, okay?"

Skeptical, I scrunch my brow. "Is that something people actually do? Or does that only work in movies and cartoons?"

"Well, it seems like you've tried just about everything else," he says with a smirk.

Fair point. I take a seat on the lid of my suitcase and it flattens a bit under my weight, enough that when Asher crouches down beside me, he can move the zipper. With a hefty tug, he manages to muscle it closed.

"You're a godsend," I tell him with a grin.

He lifts a shoulder, a warm smile pulling at his lips. "We just work well together."

Those five little words send a rush of dopamine straight to my brain. We do fit together well. In theory. But theories can be disproven. And while

I like the idea of Asher and me together way too much, I can't want anything more than what I've already had with him. There's too much at stake, both emotionally and professionally, for both of us.

I fumble for a response to break the silence, but luckily, he doesn't let me grasp at words for long.

"I guess we should get moving," he says.

I leap up to lend him a hand, and while he's putting a decent amount of weight on me as he pushes to his feet, he's noticeably more mobile than he was yesterday. Maybe he's not in mint condition, but at least I'm not sending him back to Trey more injured than when he left.

"Ready to go?" he asks, grabbing his duffel and lifting his chin toward the door.

"I guess so."

I take one last look around the room, checking for anything I may have left behind. It looks so empty with the sheets stripped off the bed and all of my stuff packed away. I wasn't expecting to be so emotional leaving a guest room, but it's felt like home for the last seven days. If not for the fact that my residency starts this week, I might be petitioning to extend our visit a little, maybe help Lolli with a few things while we work on our tans.

But duty calls. Good-bye, paradise. Welcome back to the real world.

We lug our bags down to the kitchen where the rest of the family is cleaning up the leftovers from Lolli's party and waiting to see us off. His sisters, mom, and Lolli are all stationed nearby.

"We're rolling out," Asher announces to the crew, shrugging his duffel to the kitchen floor and stretching his arms wide. "Let's get these hugs going."

And so begins the endless parade of hugs, just like when we first arrived. Only this time, I get to be a part of it.

Up first is Lolli, who squeezes me tight enough to squish my internal organs. Then I exchange social media handles with both Amber and Courtney, with promises to stay in touch. After a quick side hug from Mack and Tyson, I make my way over to Tess, who holds me good and long like I'm one of her own daughters.

By the time I finish my rounds, I'm a little choked up.

I may never be in this place or with these people again. It's an upsetting thought, but it's quickly interrupted by Tess, who seems to have an announcement to make.

"What do you think, everyone? Should we give Bailey her present?"

Everyone nods and makes noises of approval as Tess ushers me to take a seat on a bar stool. Asher must notice me nervously eyeing my suitcase, because his laugh is loud enough to cut through the hubbub.

"Don't worry, Bailey," he tells me with a smile. "There's room in my duffel for it, whatever it is."

"It's nothing big and crazy," Amber says. "Don't get her all excited."

Tess waves the comment off with a flick of her wrist and a roll of her eyes. "Oh, hush. It's the thought that counts, right? Lolli, do you want to do the honors?"

Lolli rubs her hands together excitedly as she scurries out of the kitchen, returning moments later with a shoe box decorated with red construction paper and stickers in the shape of stethoscopes and thermometers.

What in the world? I chuckle a little.

"Ta-da!" She presents it proudly with extended arms, shaking the contents with a light rattle. "Bailey's emergency kit!"

With it right under my nose, I can make out the message written in glitter glue on top: **PROPERTY OF DOCTOR BAILEY**. I choke back the lump bobbing in my throat.

"Open it up!" Nora urges me in an excited whisper. She carefully shifts a sleeping baby into Todd's arms before taking a seat on a bar stool next to mine, watching as I carefully lift the lid of the shoe box to reveal the assortment of goodies inside.

Band-Aids, gum, aspirin, protein bars, instant coffee packets, the works. They even thought to include a box of tampons, somehow managing to guess correctly on my preferred brand.

"This is too sweet, guys," I whisper, feeling my eyes begin to tear up. "You didn't have to do this."

"Of course we did," Amber says, giving Asher's shoulder a squeeze. "If not for you, we wouldn't have been able to have our brother with us this week."

"And I would've been an anxious mess the entire time Nora was in the hospital without you to calm me down," Courtney says. "You were a complete lifesaver."

I rummage through the box, impressed by how much they fit in here. There's hand sanitizer, make-up wipes, even a few seashells from the beach that Little Miss Fable proudly boasts she picked out especially for me.

When I get to the bottom, there's a stack of handwritten notes of encouragement from the whole family, guys and girls. I have to close the lid to keep from reading them right now. Better to save them for a hard day at work. Plus, I think I would get about two words into one of those notes before full-on sobbing in front of the whole Reed family.

"Thank you all so much," I manage to say, blinking away the tears pooling in my eyes. "This means the world to me."

"*You* mean the world to *us*," Courtney says. "If the people at William Simmons love you half as much as we do, you're going to have an amazing residency."

"And even if they don't, I have all the resources I need." I tap the decorated shoe box on my lap. "You guys have me covered."

"Well, I think this calls for a second round of hugs!" Lolli announces, clapping her hands.

We all laugh as if it were a joke, but moments

later, we're starting the hug parade all over again. And I don't mind one bit. I've never been much of a touchy-feely person, but I guess this family has gotten to me.

Once everyone is all hugged out, we head outside to the car and toss our bags in the back seat. The emergency kit, however, will be sitting in the front seat with me. I place it gingerly on my lap before buckling my seat belt, as I hold it in place.

"Thanks for everything!" Asher calls out the window as he throws the car into reverse.

As he backs out of the driveway, I roll my window all the way down, waving and smiling at everyone on the porch.

"Don't be a stranger!" Lolli calls to me.

The irony is real. A week ago, a stranger is exactly what I was in this house.

But now, seven short days later, I'm smiling and waving good-bye to people who feel a lot more like family, and I have no idea what to do with the emotions swelling inside me.

CHAPTER SEVENTEEN

Ghosted

Asher

"**F**inally, I catch you." My mom's voice comes over the speaker, sounding cheerful and a little relieved.

"Hey. Yeah, sorry. It's been a busy few days."

I've been cleared by the team physicians and am back to my usual schedule—which means team workouts and meetings with the coaching staff. Our season came to an abrupt and unsatisfying conclusion, as sometimes happens when you're in the semi-finals and up against the best team in the western conference, but such is life. There's always next time.

"Well, I just wanted to check on you. The doctor said the concussion is gone?"

She's referring to my text to the family, in which I told them I was given the "all clear."

"Yup. All healed up."

"That's a relief."

While I shed my towel and quickly get dressed, Mom fills me in on Nora and the baby, and Lolli's new knitting club, and some neighbor Steve's helping to structure his 401k. It's all fascinating stuff.

"That's great, Mom." I push a comb through my wet hair and eye my beard growth. I'll shave tomorrow. There's no reason not to; we aren't in the playoffs anymore. "I hate to cut this short, but I promised Covey I'd help him move today."

"Covey?" she asks. "Have I met him?"

I straighten, checking myself in the mirror. "Landon Covington. I don't think so."

"Oh, that's the rookie defenseman, right?"

"Yup."

"Okay, I know you have to go, but the reason I'm calling is to see how things are going between you and Bailey."

I pause with the comb halfway through my hair.

The short answer? They're not. I'm pretty sure she saw me as little more than a fun ride.

Does that suck? Yeah.

Am I crying myself to sleep at night? No, not exactly, but that doesn't mean I don't wish things could be different.

I've practically rubbed myself raw at the memory of our nights together. But it's not just the sex I miss—though it was off-the-charts incredible. I enjoyed our week together on the island, just hanging out and talking with her, and getting to know her away from our group of friends.

But I texted her a few days ago when we returned—just a simple message to say hi, tell her I had a good time, maybe make small talk, but she didn't even reply. If that didn't make her stance clear, I don't know what would.

"I wouldn't know," I finally answer my mom on my way toward the door.

"Hmm." Mom makes an uncertain sound, but I can tell she isn't pleased by that answer. "You guys have a connection, Asher."

"I'm not denying that."

"And don't feed me a line about being 'just

friends'." I guess she picked up on our chemistry then.

"I'm not, Mom." I grab my car keys and head toward my building's elevator. It doesn't look like this conversation is coming to an end anytime soon, and I know the guys will give me shit if I'm late.

"So, you haven't even called her since you've been back?"

"I texted. She didn't reply."

Mom makes another of those sounds. "She's a busy girl, Asher. She's just started a new job at a busy practice downtown. What exactly did this *text message* say?"

Mom has never probed about my relationship status before, but then again, Bailey is an exceptional woman. So it makes sense why my mom is suddenly so curious now.

"I thanked her for coming. Said I had a nice time. That kind of thing."

The truth is, I can recite the text from memory if I want to. I've reread it at least a dozen times, trying to figure out if I said something wrong, and then a half dozen more times in the hopes that maybe I missed her reply.

"Well, that wasn't very bright, son. You left it too vague. Too open-ended."

I chuckle. "Thanks, Mom."

Her tone softens. "I'm serious, sweetie. You didn't ask a question. Didn't give her any reason to reply."

Crap. She might be right. "And what question should I have asked?"

"You should have asked her on a date."

A sinking feeling settles low in my gut. Mom may be on to something. I'd love to take Bailey out. But that might be a pipe dream, considering she won't even respond to a text.

After hopping into my car, I tell my mom I love her and say good-bye.

The drive to Landon's is a distracted one. When I pull up in front of the high-rise complex he's moving into today, I spot Teddy, Justin, and Owen standing around a white moving truck while Landon fiddles with the lock.

"Hey, hey," Owen says when he spots me, clapping one hand on my shoulder. "How's it hanging?"

"Hey. Better. Thanks, man." Or at least that's

what I'm supposed to say. I've been cleared to play hockey again, so why don't I feel any better?

"Damn, Cali looks good on ya," Justin says, shaking my hand.

Rubbing one hand over the back of my neck, I shift my weight. "Yeah. I picked up a little tan."

Teddy offers a fist bump, which I return.

"Hey, TK."

Landon frees the lock and stands to his full six-foot-three height. I give him a nod. As we stand here in a moment of silence, I wonder if we're going to talk about the loss to Denver. But no one brings it up, and I'm not one to rub salt in anyone's wounds, so I stay quiet too. Plus, the wounds aren't just theirs—they're mine too. Even though I wasn't on the ice that night, we all suffered that loss.

"I don't have much," Landon says, "so this shouldn't take long. But I couldn't have done it alone, so thanks for coming today, guys."

"Absolutely man. That's what we're here for," Teddy adds.

Landon forces open the overhead door to the moving truck, and we all climb in.

Owen and I grab either end of a tan sofa, and so it begins.

Forty minutes later, we've moved in a dozen or so boxes, several suitcases, a wardrobe, a king-sized bed, a TV that's almost as big, and the sofa. Now we're standing in the entryway, surveying our work.

"You need a rug," Teddy says, looking over the empty-feeling apartment.

It's a large one-bedroom with a nice modern kitchen and a good view of the city. But TK's right . . . it does feel sparse, like something's missing.

Justin looks around, scratching his head. "Or a plant."

"Or a girlfriend," Owen says, and we all begin laughing.

"That last one," I say, seconding Owen's suggestion.

"If I stick around, maybe I'll work on that," Landon says.

I give his shoulder a playful shove. "You'll be here."

He didn't get much ice time this year, and

I know it worries him. He's lived out of a hotel the whole season until finally deciding to sign a lease on a pricey new apartment. And the guys are right—he definitely needs to invest in some furniture, rugs, and plants, and maybe a decent set of sheets, but I'm not going to point that out to him.

I can tell he's stressed, and I felt the exact same way at twenty-three after being drafted to my first major league team. You have no idea if it's a fluke or if it's going to work out or if you'll be cut at any second. There aren't a lot of guarantees with a rookie contract.

Still, Landon's a solid player. A little raw and undeveloped, but that'll come. I need to pull him aside later and tell him to have faith, or maybe I'll text Grant, our team captain, and give him a heads-up. He's good with heart-to-heart chats like that. I remember him taking me under his wing years ago.

"Let's order a pizza," Owen says. The dude is never *not* hungry.

Later, after a couple of large pizzas have been delivered, we head into the sparse living room with a six-pack of beer.

"Dibs on the couch," Owen calls, running over and flopping himself down into the center of the thing.

By the time the guys take their seats, Landon and I are left sitting on the wooden living room floor.

He chuckles. "Maybe I do need some more furniture."

I don't say anything, happy to eat my share of pizza and enjoy a beer with my teammates.

"So, dude, tell us," Teddy says finally, meeting my eyes with a playful glint.

"Tell you about what?" I ask around a mouthful of sausage pizza.

"About San Diego. Did you and Bailey hook up?" He wiggles his eyebrows.

"Not answering that," I say, then take another bite.

A collective wave of masculine groans fills the room as all eyes focus on me, assessing whatever it is they think happened.

"That's a yes," Owen says matter-of-factly.

"Fuck off. I don't kiss and tell."

"Holy shit, you did," Justin says, grabbing another beer.

I swallow the food I'm chewing and take a second to compose myself. "She's a cool girl, and we had an amazing time, but I don't think she'd give me the time of day in the real world."

"Why do you say that?" Owen asks before he stuffs the entire crust of his slice into his mouth.

I shake my head and grab a napkin. "Two reasons. One, she flat-out told me she wasn't looking for anything, and two, I texted her when we got back, and she never even bothered to reply."

Admitting that out loud hurts worse than I thought it would. I got ghosted—plain and simple.

Bailey never gave any indication that she'd ghost me.

That last day in San Diego was perfect. My family got her a gift, a homemade one, which everyone knows are the best kind, and she seemed truly sad to be leaving. We made a quick excursion to La Jolla on the way to the airport, where we stopped and watched the seals and sea lions that liked to sun themselves on the beach there, then we took a walk through the quaint town to grab lunch at a restaurant I liked called Cody's that I hadn't been to in years. It has a pretty balcony that overlooks the ocean that I thought Bailey might like.

She was talkative during lunch, then slept most of the plane ride back, happy to rest her head against my shoulder. When I dropped her off at home, we hugged good-bye. I never expected that to be a real good-bye, though, not with everything we'd shared. I figured we'd be making plans to see each other in a few days. Even as friends. But nope, nothing.

"That sucks," Teddy says.

I nod. "That it does. Like I said, we had fun."

"You're not usually one to give up so easily, though. So, what gives?" Owen asks.

I sigh out an exhale. "Not giving up. Just wanting to respect her space. If she says she doesn't want anything more, I have to be okay with that, right?"

"Yeah, I guess so," Owen says.

Landon lets out a loud groan. "Damn, chicks are confusing. I take back everything I said about wanting a girlfriend."

We all laugh, but my laughter sounds hollow, and I wonder if the guys can tell how much I wish things could be different between me and Bailey.

Because Bailey as a girlfriend? That would be pretty freaking amazing.

CHAPTER EIGHTEEN

Open in Case of Emergency

Bailey

O f the dozen or so internal medicine residencies I applied to, the family medicine clinic at William Simmons was by far the most competitive. The hours are so much better than working nights and weekends at the hospital, and with only two slots open each year for just over a thousand applicants, it was a long shot. A pipe dream. A best-case scenario.

And now, as of today, it's my reality. My very tiring reality.

I'm barely halfway through my first day and am prepping to see my eighth patient. I stifle a yawn as I flip through his medical records. It looks like he's just here for a standard prescription refill, so it shouldn't take more than ten minutes. Meaning I'll have fifteen precious minutes to eat lunch before my next patient. My growling stomach rejoices at the thought.

"Dr. Erickson? Your next patient is ready to see you."

I smile at my medical assistant, following her gesture toward examination room two.

Am I tired? *Yes*. Am I hungry? *Yes*. But hearing a medical professional call me Dr. Erickson makes it all worth it. I can tell that accepting this residency was the right thing, and I have a feeling these years are going to be some of the best and most rigorous of my life.

I'm in and out of the examination room within a few minutes. The medication in question, it turns out, is for seasonal allergies, so there are no complications in getting his prescription refilled. I power through the patient documentation, then hand it off to an assistant for filing.

Time to scarf down last night's leftover spaghetti and summon the energy to make it through to five p.m. When all is said and done, I'll have logged a full ten hours here today. Which can only mean one thing—I need coffee. Lots of coffee.

I head for the kitchenette and dig out my plastic

container from behind the multitude of brown bags and carryout boxes crammed on the shelves of the communal fridge. Sixty seconds in the microwave ought to do it to reheat this, just enough time for me to fire up the single-serving coffee machine that's blinking at me from the counter, indicating the water is already hot and ready to go. *Thank God.* I'm fairly confident that, through the power of caffeine, I am capable of doing anything.

Well, almost anything. Since returning from Coronado, there's been one thing that I absolutely can't do—get Asher Reed out of my head. Even now, watching my leftovers spin in the light of the microwave, my mind wanders to the barbecue nachos I made with Amber and Courtney. The look on Asher's face when he tried a bite was absolutely priceless. I could have kissed the barbecue sauce right off his lips.

Ugh. Knock it off, brain. Can I go five measly minutes without something reminding me of our California trip?

So far, the answer to that question has been a big fat *no*. The universe seems to be taking any and every opportunity it can to steer my thoughts off of my work and back to Asher.

When my first patient of the day was wearing a

San Diego shirt, I thought it was just a coincidence. But then my second appointment was with a young boy who had sustained a concussion at hockey camp. *Message received, universe.* But even the smaller things, something as innocent as the color of my bright blue scrubs, has me daydreaming about his eyes.

I can't escape it. Asher Reed is living rent-free in my head full-time, and it's emotionally draining me.

The microwave beeps, and I gather my coffee and steaming container of noodles to carry to my office. Might as well enjoy a few minutes of peace and quiet before launching into the second half of my day.

But one look at my desk, and, sure enough, my thoughts are right back to Coronado. Why? Because there's a bright red shoe box staring at me from the center of my desk. *Crap.* I forgot I brought my emergency kit with me this morning.

I heave a sigh as I plop down in my desk chair, shifting the emergency kit to the side to make room for my lunch. But I can't enjoy a single bite without my gaze venturing over to the shiny stethoscope stickers reflecting light all over my office.

I barely manage three bites before I set my fork down and dig my phone out of my purse, pulling up Asher's text from the day we arrived home.

```
Hey Bailey - Thank you again for
coming with me this week. I had
an amazing time with you.
```

A short and sweet message that I've reread a hundred times, and yet failed to respond to. But what is there to say? The week we shared was amazing, and the sex was out of this world. But now what? He has his own busy life, and I have mine.

And I'm not stupid—I know his life involves late nights surrounded by puck bunnies at the bars. I've seen the guys in action way too many times to play dumb. Whoever isn't locked down with a serious girlfriend can have his pick of any hockey groupie he wants.

Asher is no exception to that rule. In fact, his reputation of being a tough guy on the ice just makes him all the more appealing to the girls who flock to him the second he steps into a bar. I've watched him take home more than a few girls in the time I've known him.

But the Asher Reed I spent the week with at his

grandmother's house was nothing like that. He was sweet, attentive, and sensitive, always helping Lolli and Tess around the house, even when they told him that he and his injured leg should take it easy.

How could the player from the bar scene, the bad boy on the ice, be the same guy who I watched tear up at the birth of his niece, the one who confessed to me that the song "Over the Rainbow" makes him emotional? I told myself what we'd shared was fun, but very temporary. But that doesn't mean I haven't mourned the loss of his touch, our conversations, the easy laughter we shared, and more than anything, the loss of how I felt simply being around him.

I push my lunch to the side of the desk and pull the emergency kit into my lap. Yes, it's only day one, but this totally qualifies as an emergency. I'm emergency-level confused. And if there's anywhere I can find answers, it's in here.

Shifting the contents of the box aside, I fish out one of the notes of encouragement hidden at the bottom. Each piece of stationery is folded in half, hiding the message and the name of whoever wrote it, so I pick one at random, unfolding it to reveal a note in neatly scrawled handwriting.

Bailey,

You're the smartest, most beautiful girl I've ever met. Whatever it is you're dealing with, you can handle it.

xoxo, Asher

My heart leaps into my throat, but my eyes stay trained on those x's and o's. Is this a sign? A co-incidence? Whatever it is, I don't have the time to figure it out. There's a knock on my office door— it's my medical assistant again, looking at me expectantly with a clipboard in her hands.

"Your next patient is ready for you in room four, Dr. Erickson."

Already? I check my watch. *Yup.* Fifteen minutes have come and gone.

Time sure flies when you're trying not to fall in love.

CHAPTER NINETEEN

Try Not to Fall

Asher

The hollow ache in my chest hasn't gone away.

And no, it's not just because the sex with Bailey was good. Although, for the record, it was so good it could make a man want to get down on one knee and propose. Speaking of . . .

"How's the wedding planning going?" I ask Owen, needing a distraction.

We're all hanging out at Justin's place tonight. Owen moved out a while ago and into a new condo that he shares with his fiancée, Becca. Justin is hosting a little get-together tonight—there's food and beer and music playing low, kind of reconfirming his place as a bachelor pad—even though I'd bet my left nut that his girlfriend, Elise, will be moving in soon.

Owen gives me a quick nod. "It's tight. Becca and her mom are doing most of it. I tried to give my opinion once and they didn't like my suggestion, so now I'm happy 'staying out of it.'" He uses air quotes with his fingers as he says this.

"What was your suggestion?" Justin asks with a smirk before shoving a shrimp into his mouth. This ought to be good for a laugh.

"I wanted a dunk tank. Thought it'd be fun . . . mix it up, ya know? So the reception isn't so stuffy."

This earns him snickers and laughs from the guys all standing around the kitchen island. The girls are in the living room, while the guys have stayed near the food.

"Yes, because when your bride spends all day getting her hair and makeup done, the obvious thing she'd want to do next is get dunked into a tank of cold water," I say with a dry chuckle, which sends the guys into laughter again.

"Shut it," Owen grumbles. "We could have raised money for charity or something."

I roll my eyes. "It's your wedding, not a team event, dude."

"True," Owen says.

"This kinda shit is contagious, you know." Teddy waves his hand in the direction of Owen and Justin. "You're next, right, Brady?"

Justin's cool expression doesn't give much away, but his mouth twitches with a smile. "Elise is young. We're fine taking our time."

"That's cool," Teddy says with a lazy grin. "Sara and I don't necessarily want to wait, but we're also too busy to think about planning a wedding. Hell, I wouldn't be surprised if we just flew off and eloped one day."

That would fit their personalities well. They're both a little impulsive. Both a little wild. They made a freaking sex tape in college that none of us knew about. Until recently, that is.

"What about you, Landon?" I ask.

Except for me, he's the only single one left in our crew. Well, besides our captain, Grant. But Grant's a cranky bastard, and I can't really picture him settled down and being all domestic with somebody.

"Someday, for sure," Landon says. "But until the right girl comes along, I'm fine waiting."

I can't help but wonder if he means waiting, as in, well, *waiting*. Waiting to have sex. I've never seen Landon with a girl before, and the few times the guys have tried to persuade him into hooking up with a puck bunny, he turned bright red and made some excuse to take off. Then again, maybe I'm reading too much into it. Maybe he's just choosy and waiting for the right girl like he said.

"My dad was married four times," Landon says. "And after watching him go through four miserable divorces, I'd rather wait for the right girl and just do it once."

We all nod at this sentiment.

Thankfully, no one asks me about Bailey, because if they did, what the fuck would I say?

Actually, I spoke too soon, because when I wander to the fridge to grab another beer, Owen follows.

"You heard from Bailey yet?" he asks, keeping his voice low.

"Nope," I say, twisting open the top of the bottle and taking a long swig. It does nothing to ease the tight feeling in my chest.

Becca approaches the kitchen to fix herself a

plate. Owen, being Owen, bites off a chunk of a chicken wing and plants a barbeque-laced kiss on her cheek. Becca groans as she grabs a napkin and begins wiping her cheek vigorously. I chuckle as I watch their interaction.

She gives him a pointed look, an annoyed smile on her lips. "If I have to listen to you chew for one more minute, I'm going to throw you out the window."

My eyes widen. "It's good to see the romance isn't dead."

Owen only chuckles as though he's amused by this, and then swats her behind as she leaves the kitchen. "Love you too, angel." And then he goes right on eating like nothing ever happened.

But I can see he's turning over our conversation in his head. It's not over, even though I wish he'd just let it drop. There is no me and Bailey.

"Anyone heard from Bailey? Aubree, what about you?" Owen calls to the group of girls seated along the sectional.

I know what he's trying to do, and even if part of me appreciates his concern, the rest of me is a little annoyed. Bailey. Ghosted. Me—plain and simple. I should probably move on and get over it, but I'm still wallowing in denial. And Owen, being one of my best friends, can apparently smell it on me. The scent of desperation.

Aubree looks up, her expression measured as her gaze swings from Owen's to mine. She's hard to read, mostly because she's always so composed, but there's a slight twitch to her mouth.

I can't help but wonder if Bailey told her about our hookup. I'm not sure how I feel about that. Part of me hopes it was memorable enough to share with her best friend, but the rest of me wants to keep our situation private.

"I have. She's been busy." Aubree's gaze swings my way again. "She didn't come out tonight because she's not feeling well."

"Bailey's sick?" I ask, rising from my spot on a bar stool to get closer to where Aubree's seated.

Bailey probably picked up something at the new doctor's office. That place has got to be crawling with germs. I hate the idea that she's been working her ass off all week and is now too sick to enjoy the weekend. That's some fucked-up karma right there.

"She's just not feeling well," Aubree says without providing any further details.

Since Aubree isn't exactly being forthcoming with the info, I wander back over to where Owen's standing by the appetizers.

"I'm gonna go check on her," I say, my voice low.

"You sure?" Owen asks, his brow creased.

I nod. "She took care of me that week in Cali. It's only fair I return the favor, if she really is sick."

And, jeez, is it weird that part of me hopes she actually is sick and not just avoiding coming to a place she knew I'd be tonight?

He holds out his fist for me to bump. "Right on. Good plan."

I hope he's right.

• • •

Fifteen minutes later, I'm looking for street parking in front of Bailey's building. An SUV pulls out, making space, and after parallel parking at the curb, I stroll up to the door, hoping I'm not making a huge mistake.

When I ring her apartment, it takes her a minute to answer.

"Hey, it's Ashe . . . I heard you were under the weather."

"Oh. Hey," she says, her voice unsteady, followed by a long, pregnant pause.

Okay, so it's not exactly the warm greeting I was hoping for.

"Can I come up?" I hold my breath while I wait for her answer, realizing her next words mean the world to me.

"Yeah, of course. Apartment 301."

The buzzer sounds. When the front door unlocks, I head upstairs with a renewed sense of purpose.

When Bailey opens the door to her apartment, I can't help the smile that stretches my lips. She's dressed in her pajamas, and her hair is damp from the shower.

"Are you okay? Can I come in?"

She opens the door wider and motions me in.

"I heard you were sick, so I came to help. What's wrong?"

She makes a face like . . . well, like the expression you make when you stumble onto a dark corner of a porn site and see something you didn't want to see. "Do you really want to know?"

"Of course I do." I'm starting to think Bailey has no idea how I really feel about her.

"You might as well come sit down then . . . before I totally freak you out," she adds under her breath.

Totally confused, I follow her into the living room, where she sinks onto the couch and pats the seat next to her. I sit beside her, wondering what's going on.

"Are you going to fill me in, or . . ."

She inhales and lets her breath out slowly, as though she's annoyed about something. "I have anemia because of really bad periods."

I train my features so that my eyebrows don't jump up on my forehead. It dawns on me that Aubree never actually said that Bailey was sick, just that she wasn't feeling well.

"I promise that doesn't scare me off. I grew up with three sisters, remember?"

She lets out an uneasy laugh. "That's true, but still. This is a little TMI."

I take her hand and give it a squeeze. "No such thing as too much information between us."

She rolls her eyes. "I highly doubt that."

"So, are you okay?" I lace her fingers between mine and stroke the back of her hand with my thumb.

"I'm fine. It's just annoying more than anything. The medical term is menorrhagia. You can run away screaming now." She grins at me.

"Nah. I'm not gonna run away." I have no idea what she's saying, other than I'm pretty sure that once a month her vagina tries to kill her. I shift on the couch so I'm closer. "In fact, I think it's time for me to nurse you back to health, just like you did for me."

She gives me a mocking look. "Do I need to remind you that I was the one who re-sprained your groin riding you too hard?"

I laugh. "That was totally worth it, and you can do it again anytime you want. Just name the time and place."

Bailey smiles. "Stay put. I'll be right back."

While she visits the bathroom, I fire off a quick text to Owen. By the time Bailey returns, I have my game plan all ready.

"So, listen, if you want me to go, I will. But if you want to hang out for a while, I would love that too," I say. The last thing I want to do is force my company on her.

She nods, a shy smile forming on her lips. "That'd be really nice, actually."

I can't tell you how happy that one sentence makes me. "Have you eaten?"

Bailey shakes her head. "I'm starved."

"I'll order food, and then you can tell me all about your new job."

Bailey agrees, and while she opens a bottle of wine in the kitchen, I work on placing an order from the app on my phone.

"What are you in the mood for?" I call, perusing the many options.

"Anything. Seriously," she calls back. Bailey returns to the living room with two wine glasses and a shy smile. "So, how's the crew?" she asks. "Have you talked to your mom since we've been back?"

I nod, accepting the glass of red wine she hands

me. Bailey sits back down beside me and covers herself with a fuzzy throw blanket.

"Yeah, I've talked to my mom and to Nora. Everyone's good. Hannah is more adorable than ever." I show her a picture on my phone, and Bailey lets out a soft sigh.

She sips her wine, still scrolling through my pictures. There are at least a dozen of Hannah doing nothing more than sleeping, which shouldn't be all that captivating, but I get it—I'm a sucker for the photos Nora sends too. "I'm so glad I got to meet them all. It was cool to see where you came from."

Then why did you ghost me? I think, but what I actually say is, "I texted you when we got back."

She nods, frowning, and hands my phone back. "I know. I'm sorry. I've been busy, but I know that's no excuse."

"I get it. You have a full life. How's the new job? Are you liking it?"

Bailey lets out a sigh. "I do. I love it, actually. But, oh my God. The hours have been intense. Either that, or I still have a vacation hangover."

I chuckle. "I'm glad you're liking it."

She launches into a story about Dr. Simmons and I listen attentively. I could listen to this girl recite the alphabet. I love the animated way she talks with her hands, and watching her changing expressions, the passion in her eyes.

When our food arrives, I pull out the containers. "Your salad," I say, passing her the container. "I ordered you a spinach salad with steak. Hope that's okay. It has iron. That should be good for you."

She gives me a quizzical look as she accepts the container. "How did you know about the iron?"

Running one hand over the back of my neck, I hesitate. "I, uh, actually texted Owen. The dude knows everything about a woman's anatomy. I have no idea how; he just does."

Bailey smirks, forking a bite of steak. "Becca is a lucky girl."

"Hey now," I say, pretending to be offended.

She smiles at me. "If memory serves me correctly, you know your way around a woman's anatomy just fine."

Damn straight. A surge of pride rushes through me, mixed with a hint of lust. I can't help it. Anytime I think about us together . . . I get this weird floaty feeling in my chest, and my entire body aches.

"I'd be happy to give you a refresher anytime."

Bailey laughs, the sound deep and throaty. "Maybe. Just not tonight." She winks.

"Noted." I can't help the smile that twitches on my lips. Being near her makes me happy. I can't really explain it—it just does.

After dinner, we cuddle and watch a movie on the couch like it's the most natural thing in the world. And even though we're comfortably lounging on her sofa and the last thing I want to do is rock the boat, I'm dying to know.

"So, can I ask you something?"

Bailey turns her head, meeting my eyes. "Of course you can."

"I know you said you've been busy, and I'm sure you have been, but honestly, why didn't you text me back when we got home?"

Bailey weighs my words, pausing and releasing a short breath. "It was fun, right, but you don't have to do all this." She waves her hands as she says this.

Okay, now I'm confused. "Do . . . all of what, exactly?"

"Be here. Be all sweet to me. Pretend like we're more than a hookup."

Her words are like a fist to the sternum. "I'm not pretending, Bailey."

"I guess I didn't want to be in your way, cramping your style now that we're home," she adds with a shrug, and I can't ignore the way she drops her gaze to her lap.

My voice is barely a whisper when I respond. "Maybe I want you in my way."

She meets my eyes with a wry expression. "That has got to be the least romantic proposition of all time."

I chuckle, thankful that she made the move to ease the tension that was beginning to swamp her living room. "You're right. That was pretty bad. Let me try again?"

She nods, smiling. "The floor is yours. Woo me, Asher Reed."

I'm not even sure where to start, honestly. I didn't expect to come here and bare my soul tonight. But when Aubree said Bailey was sick, wild horses couldn't have kept me away.

"I liked spending time with you."

With a tilt of her chin, she nods. "I liked it too." Her voice is soft, barely above a whisper.

I can't let myself look at her mouth, otherwise I'm going to want to kiss her. And right now is about talking, not kissing.

"It's probably going to sound crazy, but I missed you this week. I got used to you being right across the hall. Got used to having you there to talk to. Used to you in my bed."

Bailey's gone quiet on me, and I have no idea what she's thinking.

"Say something," I tell her. "Whatever's on your mind. I'm a big boy; I can handle it." Even though I've just given her the go-ahead to crush me, I really hope she doesn't.

"Is it weird that I thought you were going to propose some type of friends-with-benefits thing?"

What the . . . Is that really all she thinks of me?

"Would you have said yes if I did?"

Bailey shrugs. "It's probably all I have time for."

I nod. That sucks.

"But you want more?" she asks.

"I want more." It's a statement, not a question, and my voice is sure.

Bailey grins. "I like a man who knows what he wants." She taps her chin thoughtfully.

"I want you, Bailey," I say, my tone filled with certainty, even though my heart is pounding so hard, it's banging against my ribs.

"You'll have to work for me."

"Then buckle up, sweetheart, because I'm damn good at working hard for what I want."

The sound of Bailey's laughter is like medicine for the ache that's lived inside my chest for the past week. "I think I'd like to see that."

"I like you in a way that's totally new for me, but I want a chance. I want to see where this could go, if you want that too."

Bailey's full gorgeous lips twitch. "What did you have in mind?"

My heart surges. "Let me take you out on a real date. Next weekend. Just you and me. Are you free?"

"It's a date."

I lean in, and when my lips capture hers, there's a week's worth of passion and fire poured into one searing-hot kiss.

TWENTY

Giving it a Go

Bailey

I'm sitting on a breezy brick patio with my four best friends, perusing a brunch menu as thick as a chapter of a med-school textbook. It's a rare sunny Seattle Saturday, meaning every outdoor table at this restaurant is booked all day. But thanks to Aubree, the queen of reservations, we snagged a table with only a day's notice.

"I don't know how I'm supposed to decide," Elise says, running her finger down the extensive list of skillet options. "This place is unbelievable."

"Yeah, Aubree." Becca folds her arms over her chest. "Is there a reason you were keeping the best brunch spot in Seattle a secret from us?"

A half smile tugs at Aubree's lips as she takes a

good long sip of coffee, thinking over her response. "Honestly? Because if you knew this place existed, none of you would go to Saturday morning yoga with me ever again."

"Busted," I say, raising my mug in the air. Everyone laughs, except Aubree, who pushes out her lower lip in a pout. "Kidding, babe. Yoga is fun. But, let's face it. Nothing can compete with banana bread French toast."

Sara's eyes widen in disbelief as she fumbles for her menu and flips through the pages. "Do they have that here?"

"Yup. And you'd better believe I'm ordering it. I ate healthy all week. I need a carb hit."

When the waitress appears with her pen and notepad at the ready, I agree to share my French toast with Sara in exchange for a few bites of hash browns. Once our orders are placed, Aubree gathers up the menus and passes them off to the waitress, leaving plenty of room on the wrought-iron table for her to plant her elbows and lean into full-on gossip-mode position.

"So, Bailey. What was up with Asher going over to your place when Aunt Flo had you bedridden?"

Jeez. Way to call a girl out.

I shrug. "It was nothing. He wanted to take care of me since I spent the whole week in Coronado playing doctor for him. He was just returning the favor."

According to the skeptical look on Aubree's face, that answer isn't good enough for her. "Really? Because the last time we talked about Asher, it seemed like *you* were the one who needed to *return the favor*."

The rest of the girls shoot me a totally confused look. I guess my best friend actually kept her mouth shut when I told her about what went down in San Diego. Or rather, *who* went down. I haven't filled her in yet on the fact that I did, in fact, return the favor. And then some.

"What are you talking about, Aubree?" Sara asks, getting no answers out of me, but Aubree's lips are sealed too.

I guess it's my news to share, and there's no time quite like the present.

"Asher and I," I say, then quickly realize I don't know where I'm going with this.

How many details do I really want to disclose?

This patio is packed, and the family sitting at the table next to us doesn't need to hear the details of my steamy SoCal hookup. Maybe it's best that I keep it short and sweet.

I gulp down my nerves and cut straight to the point. "Asher and I have a date this afternoon."

The table lets out a collective gasp, followed by an outburst of excited chatter, everyone insisting that they saw this coming before anyone else. I think I even hear Becca say something about Asher being my plus-one to her wedding. Give these girls an inch, and they'll take a whole mile.

"Don't get too excited." I motion for the group to simmer down, calming their excited chatter to a dull roar. "It's just a date. Nothing official yet."

"Okay, but did you guys . . . you know?" Elise wiggles her eyebrows at me suggestively. "Did something happen in California that you haven't told your girls about?"

I empty a packet of sweetener into my coffee, keeping my focus there to avoid eye contact. "A few things may have happened."

Cue the excited chattering again.

"Bailey frickin' Erickson!" Elise squeals, high-fiving me from across the table. "I am so impressed. I knew you had it in you."

"He'd better be more careful with you than he is on the ice," Becca adds on a serious note.

"He is, trust me," I tell her. "He can actually be really gentle and sweet when he wants to be. You should see him with his little cousins."

Elise claps a hand over her heart. "A guy that's good with kids? *Ugh.* I'm such a sucker for that."

"And this is a *date* date, right?" Aubree asks. "Not just a booty call?"

"Yep. A real, honest-to-God date. I thought it was just going to be a hookup to him, but . . ." I shrug again, feeling my cheeks go warm. "I guess we're going to try it out."

"Okay, so I have to be a buzzkill for a second." Sara breaks her relative silence, her brows scrunched together in thought. "Are you concerned about juggling a relationship with your residency? I worry about you getting overwhelmed."

"Trust me," I say with a sigh, "worried doesn't even begin to cover it. At this point, I'm practically a walking pros-and-cons list about starting anything serious. But . . ."

I can't finish my thought before my mind goes racing full speed back to Coronado. Every hair on my arms stood upright each time Asher's wild blue eyes met mine from across the beach. And when he came to check on me last week, all it took was seeing him at my doorstep for my heart to fall right back into place. What we have is electric, and he's willing to work to make me his. It would be a shame not to let him try.

"All right, who ordered the banana bread French toast?"

The uneasy feeling in my stomach is instantly replaced with pure hunger when the waitress sets my plate in front of me. *Holy crap*, this French toast looks like it was sent directly from heaven. One bite, and I'm convinced it was cooked by an angel.

As we eat, the conversation shifts to wedding planning, and Becca launches into some ridiculous story about her future hubby requesting a dunk tank at the reception. It's absolutely hilarious and totally something Owen would suggest, but my attention goes out the window when I feel my phone buzz twice in my purse. Just as I hoped, it's a text from Asher.

```
Hey, gorgeous, are we still on
for today at 3? I'll pick you
up.
```

Holding my phone under the table, I excitedly type out my response.

```
See you at three! I'm so ex-
                          cited.
```

I tack a smiling emoji at the end of the message, but just before I press **SEND**, I switch it to a red heart instead. It's a tiny, silly change that might not mean much. But to me, that little picture of a red heart is worth a thousand words.

Or really, just one little word that it's too soon to say.

• • •

"Down in a sec!"

It's three o'clock on the dot, and my intercom just buzzed, announcing Asher's arrival.

"Actually, two minutes!" I push on the button again, yelling into the intercom. "Just give me two minutes."

I had the whole afternoon to decide on an outfit, and now seconds before walking out the door, I'm second-guessing every choice I've made.

What do you wear for a date when you have absolutely zero clue what you're doing?

I've tried to keep my outfit as middle-of-the-road as possible. Not too fancy, not too casual. After trying on and rejecting about fifteen different outfits, I settled on my pink paper-bag shorts, mostly because they're the exact same color as my bikini that Asher drooled over the whole time we were in Coronado. Paired with a tucked-in black V-neck top and a delicate gold necklace, I look cute, but not over-styled.

So, why am I still fighting off a tidal wave of nervous energy? This is Asher. We've already slept together. Twice. Hell, he's the one who's supposed to be impressing me on this date, not the other way around.

Yet, I can't deny the lump stuck in my throat.

Knowing that he came over to care for me cracked something open inside my chest. We may have started as a casual hookup, but dare I wish for something more? The possibility both thrills and scares me.

With one final mirror check, I sigh as my buzzer goes off again. *Shit*.

Okay, no more time for second-guessing. I can't keep him waiting.

Slipping my purse over my shoulder, I head out the door and down two flights of stairs, spotting Asher the moment I step outside. One look at him, and I'm instantly calm. Partially because he's dressed casual too—he's in black jeans and a gray tee, which is stretched tight across his chest. But also because with one flash of his gorgeous smile, I forget whatever it was I was worried about.

As I make my way toward him, my breath catches as his bright blue gaze slips from mine, all the way down to my strappy nude sandals, then back up to meet my eyes again.

"Hey there, gorgeous." He flashes me another smile and, to my surprise, pulls me in for a slow, gentle kiss hello.

My heart flutters in response, even when he pulls back, giving me another appreciative once-over.

"You look cute as hell, you know that?"

My heartbeat thumps faster as I take in his compliment. "I clean up all right when I don't have to wear scrubs," I joke, tucking a loose strand of hair behind my ear. "Now, are you finally going to tell me what we're doing today?"

"Well, since I know it can be hard to return to real life after vacation, we're going to be tourists in our own city for the afternoon."

His tone is so matter-of-fact that, for a second, I almost don't realize that his answer wasn't really an answer at all. I still have zero info on what our day holds, and by the looks of it, he's not leaving room for any more questions. Lacing his fingers with mine, he tugs me toward the crosswalk and across the street to where he's parked.

Asher's shiny black sedan is easy to spot amongst the bikes and beater cars that line my street. I live in the university district, and most med-school students are a little more worried about tuition than their cars, myself included. Compared to my dumpy little sedan, his luxury car may as well be a stretch limo. Especially because he opens the passenger's side door for me like a damn limo driver.

"You don't have to do that," I say with an eye roll. "I have two quite capable hands, you know."

"Oh, I know all about your capable hands," he

says through a smug grin. "But last I checked, I'm supposed to be wooing you. So, let me be a gentleman, will you?"

I concede, sliding into the passenger's seat, noting how clean the inside of his car is. I wasn't exactly expecting smelly duffel bags—he's trying to impress me, after all—but this car looks like he could have driven it here right off the lot.

"Is this a new car?" I ask as he presses a thumb to the push start.

He shakes his head, pulling a pair of aviator sunglasses out of the console. "I just got it detailed before I picked you up."

Draping one arm around my seat, Asher shifts the car into reverse and twists to look over his shoulder, careful not to get too close to the car parked behind him.

I know it's just a practical move—he's not even touching me, after all—but that doesn't prevent the goose bumps from racing down my arms. And those don't disappear until we're a solid mile down the highway, when the bridge over the canal comes into view. It's my absolute least favorite part of going downtown.

But I've hardly registered that I'll be facing

my fears from Asher's passenger seat again, when I feel his hand resting palm-side up on my thigh, ready to offer a reassuring squeeze to my clenched hand. And despite my fear, a smile forms on my lips as I lay my hand in his, holding on tight.

"How well do you know the coffee scene around here?" he asks, a pretty obvious attempt at distracting me from the fact that we're surrounded by water on both sides.

But I don't mind. Maybe subtlety isn't his strength, but a guy who remembers that I need to be distracted while on bridges is still golden in my book.

"I spent most of med school shutting down the same coffee shop almost every night. I haven't really been anywhere else."

He lifts a brow at me from behind his aviators. "The one by Aubree's yoga studio?"

"How did you know that?"

A smirk tugs at his lips. "I did my research. I had to make sure I was taking you somewhere you've never been before. We're being tourists, after all."

Once we've cleared the bridge, I expect Asher

to put his hand back on the wheel, but he leaves it where it is, occasionally stroking my knuckles with his thumb as he steers one-handed through the streets of downtown. It's a few quick turns until he pulls the car up to the curb, parking at our destination—a weathered brick building containing one of Seattle's most popular coffee shops. Or so I've heard. I've never been.

I follow him inside and up to the counter, taking in the contrast of the bright white tile against the black bistro tables, each one surrounded by coffee drinkers sipping out of bright red ceramic mugs. It's cozy in here, and the delicious smell of fresh grounds hangs in the air like warm, familiar fog. Asher has to speak up over the whirring of the grinders to place his order.

"Two large vanilla lattes, please. Extra hot." He slips his wallet out of his back pocket, shooting me a knowing wink over his shoulder as he inserts his black card into the chip reader. "Need anything else?" he asks, but I'm too dumbfounded to respond.

How did he know my exact coffee order, right down to the temperature specifications?

"I told you I did my research," he reminds me on a whisper, squeezing my side as he drops a ten into the tip jar.

Damn. This guy is good.

The weather is too good to waste inside, so we agree to take our lattes to go and enjoy whatever the city throws our way today. I take slow, measured sips of my latte as we walk, stifling my laughter when Asher burns his tongue on the extra-hot milk. Despite his scalded taste buds, he agrees with me that this has to be the best cup of coffee within the city limits. It's the perfect mix of milk and espresso, and whatever vanilla syrup they're using has to be homemade, because it's next-level awesome.

"Can you believe I've been drinking mediocre vanilla lattes for four years?" I ask, licking foam off my lower lip. "And the whole time, I could've been drinking an actual dream in a cup."

Asher slides one arm around my waist, resting his hand on the small of my back as we walk. "Sometimes the best things are right under our noses. It just takes some time to find them."

As we make our way south down the street, hand in hand, I find myself noticing things I've never seen before. Have there always been this many murals here? Since when has there been a stationery shop on this block? With Asher at my side, wandering through Seattle feels like exploring a brand-new city.

When we pass an upscale baby boutique, he's the one who suggests we go inside and pick out an outfit for Hannah. Instantly, my heart clenches with intense feelings for this man.

We take our time in the store, perusing the adorable outfits and fuzzy baby blankets as we sip our lattes. After a little while, we agree on a precious red cashmere onesie meant for six-month-olds, meaning his baby niece will fit into it just in time for Christmas. He carries the little pink bag out of the store with pride. It's really freaking adorable, and just another tick in the pro column for Asher Reed. And, yes, there is absolutely nothing listed in the con column.

We walk for a little while longer, chatting about his family, and the team. He answers every question I have, and intersperses the conversation with questions of his own about my job and family. It's interesting how you can know someone casually for years, but never get to know them on the deep level like I'm starting to connect with him now. I want to know every single thing about him, and he's willing to give me that.

"I guess we should start heading back." I sigh, gesturing to the sun sinking low in the amber and orange sky. Just the suggestion of wrapping up our outing puts a knot in my stomach. But he suggested an afternoon date, so I'm guessing this is it.

"I've got a better idea." Asher looks over toward the shiny apartment tower just down the block. "It's a much shorter walk back to my place. And I've got a bottle of wine and a takeout menu with our names on it."

I plant a hand on my hip and give him a knowing look. "It's almost like you planned it that way, huh?"

"Yeah," he says with a smirk. "Almost."

It's a five-minute walk and a quick elevator ride up to Asher's apartment, which is as clean and polished as his car interior. While he looks for a safe place to store our present for baby Hannah, I settle into his black leather couch, admiring the expensive bottle of cabernet and two stemless wineglasses waiting for us on the coffee table. Moments later, he reappears with a wine opener and a charcuterie plate.

"So I'm guessing you had a feeling this date would go well?" I tease, nodding toward the spread.

"Can't blame a guy for being confident." He takes a seat beside me and uncorks the bottle, filling the first of the two glasses and passing it over to me.

"Did your research tell you that cab is my favorite wine?"

"Nope, that was just dumb luck." He laughs as he fills the second glass. "Let me know how it is."

I take a slow, careful sip, letting the rich velvety taste wash over my tongue. "Delicious. Although it can't compare to Lolli's special juice."

Asher laughs, a loud, deep sound that makes my heart swell. "I don't think anything could compare to Lolli's special juice. Not in alcohol content, anyway."

"Hey, if not for those drinks, I might not have made a move on you that night," I remind him as I set my glass down on a coaster, leaving my hands free to rest on his thigh. "And then where would we be?"

He shakes his head, wrapping one muscular arm around my waist and pulling me snug against him. "Trust me, gorgeous. The moment you walked out in that little pink bikini, I was a goner."

He pauses to set his wine down next to mine before pressing a gentle kiss onto the top of my head. It's sweet, delicate, and soft . . . so many things that, before our trip to Coronado, I never thought Asher Reed could be. But here, cozied up in his strong arms, feeling the rhythm of his heartbeat as it syncs with mine, I know that the bad boy from the ice is long gone.

The silence is comfortable, pleasant even, but it doesn't last long before he breaks it.

"Well?"

I blink up at him, waiting for a more complete question. "Well what?"

"How did I do? Should I consider you properly wooed?"

I tap my chin with my index finger, looking up at the ceiling. "Today *was* pretty much perfect. And you were pretty helpful when I had that rough period last week."

He gives a firm nod. "Yep. That stuff still doesn't scare me, and won't. Three sisters, remember?"

"Oh, I remember." I laugh. "Maybe you remember that your three sisters spent their whole vacation trying to set you and me up."

"They know a good thing when they see it." His tone becomes serious as his blue eyes lock with mine. "Let's face it, Bailey. We have chemistry. I know you have your doubts, but I'm crazy about you. Let's just give this thing between us a shot."

"Having chemistry isn't the same thing as being ready for a relationship, Ashe. Hell, how do I even know I want a boyfriend? I have a pretty full plate as it is."

"Then let me be your dessert."

I scrunch my nose. "What do you mean?"

"Bailey, I know you don't *need* a boyfriend. Your life is already full without one. And I have to say, I love that about you. You're not out chasing guys, trying to find your other half. You're whole on your own. So, I don't want to be your other half. I just want to be the guy on the side who gets to take you out on the weekends. And maybe the guy who gets to make you scream in bed sometimes too."

I shift out of his arms, crossing mine over my chest. "The guy on the side? Do you think I see you as some kind of side piece, Asher?"

"I don't know, Bailey. What do you see me as?"

It's a question I don't take lightly. Inhaling deeply, I organize my thoughts the best I can.

"I see you as one of the sweetest, most caring guys I've ever met," I admit on a sigh. "Not to mention totally out of my league. But I also see you as a professional athlete with a million adoring fans who could have any girl he wanted."

"But I want you, only you," he says, his voice hushed and sincere. "If you'll have me."

His words hit me like a semi-truck against my windpipe, and for a moment, I'm speechless.

He wants you, stupid. There's nothing left to analyze or overthink anymore. *All that remains is just one little question.*

Am I brave enough to set aside the pros-and-cons list and just go for it?

The answer comes out on a shaky exhale. "Yes."

His bright blue eyes flicker in excitement. "Yeah?"

"Yes. Let's do this. You and me."

The words are hardly off my lips before Asher's

mouth is crashing into mine, kissing me again and again, each pass of his tongue against mine more passionate than I've ever been kissed before. My hands find their grip on his shoulders as he tugs me into his lap, working his fingers into my hair as he tilts my head just so.

"God, you're gorgeous," he whispers between eager, hungry kisses. "I can't believe you're mine."

His fingers trail down my hip, tugging the bow of my shorts loose, like he's unwrapping a perfect present. Before he can shimmy them down over my hips, I stop him, gripping his wrist in my fingers.

"What about your car?" There's genuine concern in my voice, but Asher just smiles.

"For all I care, they can tow it." He laughs, shaking his head as he runs his thumb along my lower lip. "I've got everything I need right here."

He kisses me then. Really kisses me. Like it's a foregone conclusion that I'm already his.

TWENTY-ONE

No Regrets

Asher

One month later

I don't like this. But being away from Bailey for three days is going to be my norm soon, once the season starts up, so I guess this is good practice. I thought I had more time with her this summer, but when Coach Dodd asked me to attend the training camp for our minor league affiliate team in Wisconsin, I couldn't exactly say no.

Which means I'm currently standing in the center of a foul-smelling locker room, watching twenty dudes lace up their skates. I call out for their attention and check the notes I took on my phone after watching their practice yesterday.

"Listen up!" I shout when the back of the room

still hasn't quieted down. Silence finally settles around us, and all eyes swing up to meet mine. "Things got off to a slow start yesterday, but once you were warmed up, you were on. Let's get there faster today. You hear me?"

"Yes, sir!" they shout in unison. Their coach has trained them well.

"Benson, you need to look for passing opportunities. Crosby, a defenseman's job is to watch the players, not the puck. Doing so will help you find spots for turnovers. And everyone else, skate faster, push harder, no mercy. That's what I want to see today. Got it?"

"Yes, sir!" they shout again.

As I watch them shuffle from the locker room and out onto the ice, I'm hit with a feeling of pride. Knowing that I could play some small role in helping them to become better hockey players, better competitors—hell, maybe even better men—it lights a fire in me I didn't know was there before. I realize that coaching could be a pretty neat gig down the road when I retire from playing.

Maybe that's why Coach Dodd sent me here this week. Who the hell knows? Then again, maybe he sent me so I would appreciate how nice our training facility is compared to this shit hole, because *holy hell*. I'll never take our dressing room for granted ever again.

Metal benches and cheap folding chairs are scattered around the room, along with piles of battered equipment. It kind of makes our locker room look like a luxury hotel with its sleek polished-wood benches and built-in cabinets for each player, where our jerseys and equipment are cleaned and hung for us at the start of every practice and every game.

After the guys have warmed up on the ice, the coach blows a whistle and organizes the teams for a scrimmage.

I stand beside the assistant coach and pull out my phone to take more notes as I prepare to watch them play today, but a text message from Bailey distracts me.

I'm stressing. I don't know what to wear to this banquet-thingy.

I smile down at my phone, my thumbs already working to type out a quick message before the team's leadership realizes I'm texting my girlfriend rather than paying attention to the game.

Bailey and I have only been officially dating for a month, but I already can't imagine my days without her. She just makes me happy. And the banquet-thingy she's referring to is the official kickoff to our season where our team leadership treats the team and their significant others to a fancy dinner out before the madness of the season begins. I'm really freaking stoked that Bailey's agreed to accompany me. Every other year, I've gone solo.

Baby, you could wear a damn garbage bag and still look good.

You're sweet, but you're wrong.

I chuckle and quickly work to type out another message.

Maybe ask Elise if she has something you can borrow. She's been to a million of these things over the years.

I'm about to pat myself on the back for actually having a good suggestion until I see Bailey's reply.

Um . . . no. You do realize Elise is like three sizes smaller than

```
me, right?
```

My eyebrows draw together. No, I didn't realize that. Bailey's body is freaking perfection, curvy
and generous and lovely. I never stopped to consider what size she wears—because it doesn't matter.

```
Whatever size you are, that's
        the perfect size to me.
```

I hope my reply smooths over me just putting
my foot in my mouth. I'm about to add that if she
wants to go shopping for a new dress, I will happily sit in the dressing room and watch as she tries
gown after gown, but the team's aggressive right
winger slams into the glass in front of me, and I'm
so distracted that I startle and the guy besides me
starts laughing.

Smiling, I shove my phone in the pocket of my
jeans and direct my attention to the ice.

• • •

Damn. My breath sticks in my lungs, and I make an
inarticulate sound.

"Ashe?" Bailey squints at me from beneath her
thick mascara-coated lashes. She's probably not
sure if I'm choking, or maybe having a seizure. It

could be both. "I said, do I look okay?" she repeats, slower this time.

"You look incredible." I try again, a huge grin overtaking my face. "All the guys are going to be jealous when I show up with you on my arm."

Bailey's laughter is the best sound. She's been working too much and I haven't seen enough of her. "You're ridiculous."

I give my finger a twirl. "Do the thing."

She spins in a slow circle, obviously humoring me since her mouth is pressed in a line. But her eyes are amused.

"Damn, babe." I whistle low under my breath.

Her dress is hunter green, the exact shade of our team's jerseys, and it's fitted down to the knee, hugging every last one of her curves. It's sexy, but still totally classy. I've never seen a more perfect sight.

"Shall we do it?" she asks, her tone happy.

"Absolutely. Let's roll."

I help Bailey into the passenger side of my car, and it's a quick ride to the restaurant where our team dinner is being held tonight. In the past, I've always attended this event alone, but tonight it'll be nice having Bailey on my arm.

When we arrive at the restaurant, I leave my car with the valet, and then Bailey and I are led into a private dining room in the back of the building. With one hand on Bailey's lower back, I adjust my tie with the other.

We pause just inside the elaborately decorated private dining room to get our bearings. There are three long tables, probably a dozen chairs at each one, and a couple of my best friends from the team are seated at the middle one. I see Owen and Becca, Justin and Elise, and Teddy and Sara. Grant, our captain, is here alone, sitting beside Coach Dodd at the first table. At the farthest table near the windows, Morgan is sitting with a girl I've never seen before, whispering in a low conversation.

"Asher, over here," Coach Dodd says, motioning me over to the coaches' table. "I want to hear about your trip to Wisconsin."

Smiling, I escort Bailey toward the table where we'll apparently be sitting with Grant, coaches Dodd and Bryant and their wives, and a couple of other players. But I don't miss the way our second line's left winger, an asshole named Jason Kress, visually molests Bailey when we stop beside the table.

Fucker.

"This is my girlfriend, *Doctor* Erickson," I say, gesturing toward Bailey.

She gives me a weird look. "It's *Bailey*. Hi, nice to meet you all."

"What?" I ask innocently. My girlfriend is a doctor, and I'm damn proud of that fact.

After the introductions are made and our drink orders have been placed, we settle into easy conversation. I'm pleased to see Bailey can hold her own, chatting casually with my head coach and his wife. Not that I'm surprised by this. Bailey handles herself like a champ in any situation I've thrown her in—and that includes when we stayed with my family for an entire week.

She's incredible, and it's just one more thing I appreciate about her. Soon, she has the whole table laughing with an entertaining story about an elderly patient who thought he was allergic to gluten but actually just had gas. I find myself chuckling along too, mesmerized by her.

I guess I didn't realize, but this is the first time our friends are seeing us out together as a couple, and they're not exactly being inconspicuous about their glances over at us. Owen's got a huge smile plastered on his face, Justin is watching us closely like he's looking for signs I'm going to fuck this up, and Teddy's face is scrunched up like he's trying to figure out how exactly this happened without him knowing about it.

We dine on perfectly cooked steak and giant prawns swimming in some type of butter sauce. During dinner, I learn yet another perk of having a girlfriend—when she's full and insists she can't eat another bite, I get to polish off the rest of what's left on her plate. It's freaking awesome. Who knew there were so many fringe benefits to monogamy? I might have signed up for this a whole lot sooner had I known.

Actually, that's a lie, because somehow I think the universe, or whoever is in charge was waiting until I was ready, and then put Bailey in front of me at exactly the right moment.

After our meal, I decide it's time to mingle, or at least time to put my friends out of their misery. Their curious glances and whispers still haven't stopped.

"Hey, guys," Bailey says with a little wave as we stop beside the table where the majority of my teammates are seated.

"I love your dress," Sara says to Bailey.

"Thanks." Bailey smiles.

Teddy cracks his knuckles and leans back from the table. "Let's cut to the chase, kids. Care to tell us how this all came to be?" He gestures between Bailey and me with a serious expression.

I guess I should have known this was coming.

"We had an amazing time in California, and things just kind of blossomed from there," I say, hoping that explanation is adequate.

"Did you just say the word *blossomed*?" Teddy asks, blinking at me.

Owen chuckles into his fist. His fiancée, Becca, quickly elbows him in the ribs, and his laughter turns into a sharp coughing sound.

"I think it's amazing, and it makes perfect sense, if you think about it," Elise says with a smile. "You're both incredible . . . and together? Holy power couple."

"Thank you, Elise," I say, grinning down at her.

Bailey lets out a laugh. "You guys should have seen your faces at dinner. It was like you've never seen Asher with a girl before."

"We haven't," Owen says matter-of-factly, watching us with a blank stare.

Well, that certainly isn't true. I've gone home with my fair share of puck bunnies over the years, but thankfully, no one brings that up. It's not exactly the mental image I want my new woman to be left with as the evening comes to a close. I'm hoping to get lucky tonight, after all.

Wanting to change the subject, I look over at Bailey and say, "Ready to get out of here?" I'm leaning close, close enough that the sweet smell of her floral shampoo makes my heart gallop.

She flashes me a shy smile. "Sure. Let's do it."

After a round of good-byes, and one last story from Bailey about the practice where she works, which leaves Coach Dodd rolling with laughter, we're finally off. And it doesn't come a moment too soon, because I can't wait to be alone with her.

I can't imagine that feeling ever fading because, this girl? She's everything to me, and there's no way in hell I'm going to miss my shot at something real.

• • •

Back at my place, we've just moved this party into my bedroom. My jacket is on the floor at the foot of my bed, along with Bailey's discarded high heels.

I know I shouldn't rush this, but I'm so damn eager for her it's hard not to. Bailey's kissing my neck, and her slender fingers are unbuttoning my pants.

"Go slow, baby. We have all night," I say, tipping her chin up toward mine so I can capture her lips in a soft kiss.

"You're right." She grins up at me. "And there's no one to interrupt or overhear us either."

"Exactly. So, feel free to be as loud as you want."

"Ashe . . ." She moans when my hands drift from her waist up over her full breasts.

"I love the way you say my name," I say on a sigh.

But that perfect moment is interrupted by my phone vibrating loudly against the dresser where I've placed it. *Dammit.*

Bailey pulls back, meeting my eyes. "Do you want to get that?"

Not even a little bit. "Ignore it." Unfortunately the vibrating doesn't stop. "Hold that thought," I tell Bailey with one last kiss. Grabbing my phone, I see its Landon's number. "Yeah?" I answer, more than a little annoyed.

"Heyyy, Asher," he says a little too loudly. "Good thing you picked up."

"What's up, man?"

"I need a ride. Had a little too much to d-drink," he says.

"Can't you just call an Uber?"

"No can do," he says, voice unsteady. "Wasn't there something in the rookie orientation about public intoxication being the top of coach's no-no list?"

Well, the bastard's right, but why do I have to be the one to bail him out? Doesn't he know I'm finally about to be naked with the woman I've been craving for three days?

"Can you call someone else? I'm kinda in the middle of something."

Bailey gives me a strange look. "It's Landon," I mouth.

She nods.

"I already tried Justin, Owen and Teddy. And there's no way in fuck I'm calling Grant."

I sigh. He's right. Our team captain Grant would have his balls at the next practice if he called him drunk in the middle of the night. "Where are you?"

"Downtown. The Pink Elephant or something. Maybe it's the Purple Pachyderm." This sends him into a fit of laughter.

"Text me the address. I'll be there in ten minutes."

"Sweet. Thanks," Landon slurs before ending the call.

"What's going on?" Bailey asks the moment I grab my keys from the dresser and button my pants.

"Looks like we're going to pick up a drunk rookie."

Her eyes widen. "Oh, fun," she says with sarcasm.

Like a root canal.

We retrieve Landon from the bar downtown where he's waiting for us on the curb, and ten minutes later, we're helping him inside his dark apartment.

"There, there, buddy." I tap him on the shoulder. Bailey gives me a look that says, *you can do better than this, dude.*

Dammit I planned to be balls-deep inside of my girlfriend right now, not watching over a drunk ass rookie on the team.

"Do you think you're gonna be sick?" I ask, following him further inside the apartment.

He shakes his head. "Just hungover as fuck in the morning."

I nod. "That sounds about right. Come on then, let's get you to bed."

Bailey takes one side, and I take the other, steering the awkward, lumbering, six-foot four-inch Landon to his bedroom at the end of the hall.

Once inside, he works on unbuttoning his dress shirt while Bailey announces she's going to get him a glass of water. He stumbles sideways, leaning one hip against the dresser.

He's still fumbling with the buttons on his shirt when she returns. With a sigh, Bailey sets down the glass and then crosses the room to stand in front of Landon.

"Let me help," she says gently, unfastening each button until he's free and can shrug off the dress shirt. He flings it ungracefully to the other side of the room.

Even drunk Landon knows neither me nor Bailey is going to help free him from his pants, so he falls back into the bed still wearing the dress pants he wore to the banquet. It won't kill him to sleep in them.

He lets out a loud belch and out of the blue asks, "Do you think I'd have a shot with Aubree?"

Bailey and I both chuckle. "In this state? No dude."

"But in general?" he asks, laying back against the pillows.

Bailey and I exchange a look. "I'm sure she'd love to go out with you sometime," she says after a few moments of awkward silence.

The truth is, I have no idea of Aubree would be interested in Landon. She's thirty to his twenty-three and she's career-focused and driven. Though it would be fun to watch him try to win her over.

"Get some sleep, buddy." Turning off the lights, I bring my hand to Bailey's lower back, guiding her toward the door.

"One more thing," Landon says.

"Sure," I say with gritted teeth.

"Actually, it's a question for Bailey."

"What's up?" she says, tone much more friendly than mine would have been.

"What's the main thing that a woman is attracted to in a man?"

"Oh, um, that's a good question." Bailey falters, but only for a second. "Well it depends on the woman, of course, but I guess I would say emotional strength."

"What?" Landon and I both ask at the same time.

Bailey chuckles. "Someone who is strong, someone who is, you know, going to be there for you when the going gets rough."

"Oh," Landon says. "Thanks, I guess, Bailey."

"Alright man, you good?"

Landon sighs. "Can you guys just stay a little while? I don't want to be alone."

"Sure," Bailey says cautiously.

I give her a pleading look.

"We can sit on the couch for a little while until he falls asleep," she says, quieter this time.

I flip on the lamp in the living room and Bailey and I sink down onto the couch.

Bringing one arm around Bailey, I pull her close and press a kiss to the top of her head. "Sorry about this. I know it's not how you planned on spending your evening."

She pulls back to meet my eyes. "No, it's not. But you're a good friend, Ashe."

I lean in and give her a slow, sweet kiss. Bailey's lips part and I can't resist tasting her, my tongue making a confident pass over hers.

"Can we go yet? I need you," I murmur.

"Not yet. But I have an idea about how we can pass the time." The mischievous gleam in Bailey's eyes is unexcepted, and so is the way my body temperature rachets up a few degrees.

When her hand moves to the button on my pants, I suck in a ragged inhale. "What about Landon?"

Her gaze flits over to the bedroom as her mouth lifts in a crooked grin. "I'm sure he's passed out by now. He'll be asleep for the night."

"That's true…"

With a wicked smile, Bailey slides to her knees in front of me and my chest shutters.

"Here?" I ask.

She gives a me a sultry look that makes it impossible to say no to her.

• • •

Back at my place, Bailey and I quickly pick up where we left off.

"Let's never speak of that again," I say, mouth moving to her neck. I still can't believe Landon interrupted us like that—talk about awkward.

"Deal," she pants, pushing her chest into mine.

Slowly lowering the zipper on her dress, I help her step out of it. She's so sexy, I swear my knees feel a little weak.

"What am I going to do once the season starts back up?" I ask, admiring her curves with one hand against her waist, the other touching her cheek.

She gives me a serious look. "I don't know. What are you going to do?"

I think she's asking if I'm going to dick around and break her heart. I'd kick my own ass before I let that happen. Not to mention, my mother and Lolli would probably fly across the country and castrate me.

"I'm going to miss you." I kiss her. "All the time." Another kiss.

She pulls back, still watching me, weighing my words.

"Trust me. I had enough fun when I was younger. I know what I want. And you're it."

Bailey softens, her fingers now working in earnest on the front of my pants. When she finally frees me from them, I'm heavy and hot and hard, and aching for her. Moving to my bed, she shimmies a pair of tiny black panties down her legs and removes her bra, tossing them over the side.

God, she's beautiful. And she's all mine.

"You going to stand there all night staring, or are you going to join me?" she asks, lobbing a smile at me.

"That's a damn pretty sight—you in my bed."

Impatient, Bailey curls her finger, beckoning me forward. I kick off my pants and boxers in one less-than-smooth motion while she giggles.

But just before I join her, I pause. I almost forgot. "I've got something for you."

Her expression is curious. Grabbing a folded sheet of paper from my desk, I hand it to Bailey, who's now propped herself up on one elbow to see what I'm up to. Her lips move as she reads silently, and then those gorgeous big brown eyes meet mine.

"You did this? For me?"

I nod. The paper is a health report confirming I'm STD-free.

"That was really thoughtful of you." She folds the paper and hands it back to me. "And I say that both as your doctor, and as your girlfriend."

I laugh and join her on the bed, pulling her into my lap. Bailey fits against me like she was made just for me. Her knees are on either side of my hips, and her chest brushes mine. I press my thumb against her cheek, stroking as I gaze down at her.

"No pressure either way, but I'll let you decide if you still want to use one of those." I tip my chin toward the mega-sized box of condoms we've been plowing our way through for the past month.

Bailey doesn't take her eyes from mine. "That was a very considerate gift," she murmurs. "I think I know just how to reward you."

While my heart pounds erratically, she lifts up on her knees, finding the right angle, and joins us—sinking down so slowly, my entire body shivers. Her fingernails bite into my shoulders as she clutches me, and a low whimper pushes past her lips. She moves in a slow, teasing rhythm, and it's suddenly hard to breathe.

A low groan pours out of me, and my hands tighten on her ass, holding her in place. "Maybe this was a bad idea."

Her eyes flash on mine. "Why?"

"Because I didn't know it would feel this good. I'm gonna disgrace myself."

She watches me with a hooded gaze. "You've never done this before?"

I shake my head, saying in a strained voice, "First timer."

Then Bailey brings her mouth to mine and kisses me until I forget about everything else, because *damn*, it really is *that* good.

Afterward, we lie together in a warm, cozy heap. Bailey uses my chest as her pillow, and I trail my fingers up and down her spine while my heart rate slows.

My cuff links are on the dresser, resting beside a pair of Bailey's earrings. There's something about that sight that brings a smile to my lips.

Maybe it's because I resisted the idea of this for so long—being someone's plus-one. But the reality of it is so much better than I ever dreamed. I have someone to call when I've had a hard game. Someone to laugh and cuddle with. Someone to share life's big moments with. I'm falling hard and fast, and that should probably scare me, but so far, it doesn't.

Sometimes the best things in life are the ones you never saw coming. And Bailey in my life is absolutely one of those things.

EPILOGUE

Bailey

The next summer

Is there a word for the warm, fluttery feeling you get in your chest when you're exactly where you're meant to be? Because that's what I feel when Asher turns our rental car down Lolli's street. The sound of the ocean waves crashing in the distance is as sweet and familiar as a favorite song. Even though I've only been to Coronado Island once before, the second that light-yellow beach house comes into view, I feel like I'm home.

Everything looks just as we left it last year— same pink shutters, although I think they've gotten a fresh coat of paint, same purple flowers blooming in the front flower beds, and the same big, happy family on the porch, ready to welcome us. But a lot has changed in one short year.

Namely, the fact that instead of coming to Coronado as Asher's medical supervision, I'm joining him for Hannah's first birthday party as his girlfriend.

"About time you showed up!" Lolli calls through cupped hands as we step out of the car. "You almost missed the cake!"

"I'll grab our bags," Asher says, giving my cheek a kiss and my butt a quick tap, the second of which I'm hoping his family didn't see. "You go start in on the hugs."

The second I step up onto the porch, Tess nabs me, squeezing me in her arms before passing me off to Lolli, who, at eighty-six years old, somehow manages to lift me off the ground when she hugs me tight.

"I'm so glad you could make it, sugar," she says as she sets me safely back on two feet. "We missed you so much."

"Hey, what about me?" Asher asks, feigning offense as he hitches our bags up over one muscular shoulder. "Am I just the pack mule?"

Lolli rolls her eyes, throwing her arms wide

and wiggling her fingers at her grandson. "Oh, hush. Come here, you. I watch you on TV every week. It's not every day I get to see Bailey."

"And I know a few other people inside who are excited to see you too." Tess tilts her head toward the door, which is decorated with teal streamers and a sign that reads **SEA WHO'S TURNING ONE!**

Even though the door is closed, I can still hear the low rumble of music and chatter coming from inside. If Hannah's first birthday party is anything like Lolli's eighty-fifth, I'm guessing the house is packed to the gills. And a year ago, that scared me shitless. But my days of being overwhelmed by Asher's massive family are long gone. Now I'm itching to go inside and see the people who have quickly become my second family.

Once Lolli releases Asher from her vise grip of a hug, Tess presses a kiss to his scruffy cheek and takes our bags onto her shoulders. "I'll take these up to your room. But I'll warn you, Hannah's crib is in the room next door. So if a crying baby wakes you up . . ." She puts her hands up in front of her in surrender. "Don't blame me, blame the birthday girl."

Lolli gasps, her eyes widening at the mention of the little one we're celebrating today. "We're going to miss the smash cake! *Ándale, ándale!*" She scurries through the front door like a crab into its burrow, with Tess following close behind her.

"Did she just say *smash cake*?" I cock my head toward Asher, looking for an explanation, but he just smiles and laces his fingers through mine.

"She sure did. Come on, gorgeous. Let's go see."

One step through the front door, and suddenly, I feel less like I'm at Lolli's place and more like I'm inside a craft blog brought to life. Bunches of light blue balloons are arranged in every corner to look like bubbles, and the green streamers taped to the walls make some convincing seaweed. The icing on the cake is, well, the cake itself, which is on display on the kitchen island. It's decorated to look like a treasure chest with gold chocolate coins pouring out.

"Sheesh." Asher whistles, craning his neck to take in the décor. "This seems like a lot of work for a party that Hannah won't even remember." The second the words come out, he shoots me a nervous sideways glance. "Don't tell Nora I said that."

I mime locking my lips and throwing the invisible key over my shoulder. "Your secret is safe with me."

"Did somebody say secret?" Courtney appears out of nowhere, a marshmallow bar in the shape of a seashell in her hand. "I thought you two were done keeping secrets around here."

"Nice to see you too, sis," Asher says with a smirk. "And no, no secrets. None you need to hear about, anyway."

"Are you sure?" She holds up her left hand, giving her ring finger a wiggle. "Do you guys have something to tell us?"

My gaze darts over to Asher, expecting to see his eyes bug out of his head, but to my surprise, he's pleasantly calm. There's even a soft smile tugging at his lips.

"How about we let her finish her residency before we start talking next steps?"

My heart does a quadruple backflip in my chest. So I'm not the only one who's been thinking about next steps. Noted.

"Well, if it isn't my favorite couple." Amber emerges from the crowd, pressing one hand against her heart. "Have I mentioned you two look perfect together?"

"Not since the last time we video chatted," Asher says, pulling her in for a hug. "How've you been?"

"I'm better now that you're here," she says, pinching off a bite of Courtney's marshmallow treat and popping it between her lips. "I've spent the last hour trying to keep Brooke away from Hannah's stack of presents. Whoever thought it would be a good idea to give sugar to a three-year-old is officially my enemy."

"Speaking of which, is there a spot for the cards?" I ask, fishing the bright blue envelope out of my purse.

As if on cue, the birthday girl's dad appears, giving Asher a clap on the back with one hand and snagging the envelope with the other. "I can take that. Thanks for coming, you guys."

"That money is for your daughter's college fund, Todd," Asher tells him. "No blowing it on beer and takeout, all right?"

Todd laughs, putting one hand up like he's taking an oath. "I swear it's in good hands with me. Now with Nora, you're at risk of it being used on more sparkly headbands she doesn't need."

"Come on, everybody!" a voice that is unmistakably Lolli's hollers above the chaos. "We're about to do the cake!"

The crowd gathers around baby Hannah's high chair, which is decorated with streamers that match the sparkly teal bow on her headband. She looks as cute as a button in her mermaid shirt and tutu. With her big baby blues and shock of blond hair, she could almost pass as a teeny, tiny Asher.

That thought should scare me, but instead, it brings that warm, fuzzy feeling back to the center of my chest. Just like Courtney said last year— there's always room for one more in the family. But that's a long way away. For now, I'm enjoying the feel of Asher's muscular arm wrapped around my waist, tugging me flush against him as he kisses the top of my head.

"I'm glad you're here," he whispers, squeezing me tight.

"Of course I'm here." I sink back into him, loving the feel of his strong arms around me. And I've never been so sure that there's nowhere else I'd rather be right now.

"I love you," he says, meeting my gaze.

Little tingles travel through me at his words. It's not the first time he's said them, but somehow it

286 | KENDALL RYAN

still feels a little surreal. "I love you too," I whisper back, my chest a little tight.

"On the count of three!" Lolli calls out, waving her hands in the air like a conductor. "And a-one, and a-two, and a-three!"

On her cue, the whole family bursts into the loudest, most off-key version of "Happy Birthday" I've ever heard, featuring the high, squeaky voices of Mack and Tyson, who have been having a little too much fun with the helium balloons.

"Happy birthday to youuuu!"

As we all cheer, Nora removes the unlit candle from the top of Hannah's blue-frosted cake. "All right, Hannah. Have at it!" She gestures at the dome-shaped sugary goodness in front of her.

Hannah blinks at her mama, then at her dad, and finally gives the cake a suspicious poke, sinking one tiny finger into the frosting. We all let out a collective "aww," which makes little Hannah do it again.

"The idea is for her to smash it," Asher says, pulling his phone from his pocket to snap a picture. "But I guess Little Miss Manners isn't about that life."

As if to prove him wrong, Hannah releases a loud, joyous squeal and presses an open hand straight into the cake, grabbing a handful of goopy blue frosting to shove into her mouth, and earns a triumphant cheer from the crowd.

"Never mind." Asher laughs. "I take it back. She's pretty boss."

Once Hannah's face is sufficiently covered in frosting, Lolli cuts into the treasure chest cake, and I volunteer to pass out slices. It's a good opportunity to make sure I greet everyone individually. After discussing second grade with Fable, brainstorming second birthday party themes with Todd and Nora, and recapping my first year at the medical practice to Steve and Tess, I settle in on the couch next to Asher with an extra-large slice of chocolate cake as a reward.

"You've been doing a lot of socializing," Asher murmurs into my ear, his hand floating over to my thigh, which he gives a firm squeeze. "Maybe we should, you know, head up to the bedroom for a bit. Get some *rest*."

His gaze latches onto mine with a look I know all too well. I watch as his eyes shift from bright blue to a stormy navy, a sure sign that dirty thoughts are running rampant. I can't stop the helpless shiver that races through me.

"Now?" I whisper, wide-eyed. "With your whole family down here?"

A devilish smile twitches across his lips. "What can I say? I like a challenge."

"Yeah, I learned that a year ago when you won me over."

I lean in to kiss him, my skin pebbling with goose bumps when he nips flirtatiously at my lower lip before pulling away. Damn, this man knows exactly how to turn me right the fuck on, even in the middle of a family birthday party.

"So . . . bedroom?" he growls, his hooded eyes flickering.

Before I can steady my breath enough to reply, he stretches his arms over his head in an exaggerated, obviously fake yawn.

"I think Bailey and I are going to rest up a bit before the bonfire tonight," he announces to no one in particular, and I just barely hold back a laugh.

"Yeah, I'm beat," I say, supporting his case. When in Rome, right? Or in this case, when in Coronado.

"Go take a cat nap," Lolli suggests in passing. "We'll need you well rested to help Fable roast marshmallows without setting the beach on fire."

"Great idea, Lolli." Asher's voice is sugary sweet as he pushes to his feet, offering me a hand. "Shall we?"

I place my hand in his, enjoying the trail of goose bumps chasing up my arm. "We shall."

And five minutes later, we do.

Hard and fast and wild, and better than ever before.

Asher

I've never gotten naked this fast in my entire life, but Bailey seems completely uninterested in foreplay. Which is fine by me. More than fine, actually.

As I stand with my back to the door, she palms my cock, sliding her fingers over me, and I let out a grateful sound.

"Quiet," she says, bringing a finger to her lips.

"Yes, ma'am," I whisper, pushing her panties—

the last scrap of clothing between us—to the floor.

Seconds later, we're on the bed kissing. And when she parts her thighs, I kneel between them. I can't help but notice the way she admires me. Her gaze lingers on my broad chest, then slowly sinks to my chiseled abs and then back up to my face.

I smile. Bailey grins back.

And then I'm grinding against her, only to discover she's already wet. Bailey makes a low sound in her throat.

"Shh." I place my hand over her mouth at the same time that the first slow thrust of my hips pushes my hardness slightly into her soft heat.

Bailey's eyes widen and lock on mine, and then begin to sink closed as pleasure washes over her features.

I press in deeper, and she whimpers. I know I should, but I can't bring myself to go slow. Driving my hips forward, I close all the remaining distance between us. I have to bite my lip to hold in a groan.

Bailey feels incredible. Tight and wet and hot. It's heaven. Only adding to this moment is the illicit and clandestine nature of us sneaking off early to fuck like rabbits in my room.

"Ashe . . ." She pleads with her eyes when I move my hand.

"Gonna be quiet for me while I make you come so hard you want to scream my name?" I whisper this and other filthy things into the soft, sweet skin of her throat.

Bailey makes a helpless, pleasure-filled sound that vibrates in the room, and I place my hand right back over her mouth.

I give my head a little shake. "That's not gonna work, sweetheart."

Can't have my freaking grandma hear me banging my girlfriend. Talk about an awkward walk of shame in the morning.

I'm deciding if it would be uncool to place a pillow over her head when Bailey gives my chest a shove. I move off her, already missing our connection. I think she's about to tell me this isn't going to work when she sits up, but then her legs swing over the side of the bed and she's on the move, heading toward the small attached bathroom and giving my hand a tug.

I obviously follow her, my throbbing erection bobbing with each step. And there's zero time to feel awkward about this, because my hot-as-sin girlfriend is tugging me inside the space and hoisting herself up on the counter. When she parts her knees, I kick the door closed behind me and then my mouth is hot on hers. Her tongue strokes mine as I enter her again.

My knees buckle at how good she feels.

Planting her hands on the counter, Bailey rocks her hips closer to mine, grinding up against me.

"Baby . . . you're gonna make me lose control." My voice is a desperate plea.

"Do it," she says, breathless.

"Not until you come all over me."

She gasps and meets my eyes. "I'm close."

The feeling of her bare is indescribable. I know I'm not gonna last, but I force myself to breathe, and somehow I hold out.

Bailey's hands leave the marble countertop, and then they're gripping my ass, pulling me closer as she cries out. "There."

"Yes, beautiful," I murmur, kissing her temple as she starts to tremble. "That's it."

Wildly, recklessly, she falls apart, shivering as she clings to me, her arms around my neck now, her lips pressed against my throat. The amount of trust and love flowing between us is so big, so powerful, there's not a word for it.

I can't last. And not just because of how amazingly hot the sex is between us, but because I can feel her all the way down to the furthest depths of my soul.

Moments later, I spill inside her in hot, wet bursts. I'm wrecked and sweaty and totally breathless, so it takes me a second to realize Bailey is laughing.

"What is it?" I ask, carefully withdrawing.

She's laughing harder now. "We just had sex in a flipping bathroom while we hid from your family."

"So what?"

"So, that's insane is what."

I shrug and grab her a wad of tissues. "It worked out."

She swats at me, smiling as she accepts the tissues to clean between her legs. "You're crazy."

"Crazy about you," I say with a grin.

• • •

The next morning I pour myself a mug of coffee and join Bailey at the kitchen table.

It's another beautiful day in paradise, and I'm grateful we get to spend the week here, vacationing together. I told Bailey we could have gone anywhere—any exotic location she wanted in the world—but she chose here, my grandmother's house, insisting we couldn't miss Hannah's big day. I swear it made me fall a little deeper in love with Bailey, if that were even possible.

"You sleep okay?" I ask her, enjoying the view of her sleep-mussed hair and the sight of her in my oversized T-shirt.

"You wore me out," she murmurs, giving me a soft look from across the table. It makes my body heat up a few degrees.

A few seconds later, Lolli wanders into the kitchen, settling herself in besides Bailey.

"I slept like the dead last night. You guys were so quiet up there," she says, looking between Bailey and me like she's amused by something. Or maybe she's trying to feel us out to see what actually happened after we went up to bed at such an early hour.

I shrug. My gaze flicks to Bailey's, and her lips twitch with the secret knowledge of what we did last night. We were only quiet because of how creative we got when I fucked her brains out.

Mission accomplished.

"What's on the agenda today?" Bailey asks, rising from her chair to refill her coffee. I suspect she's just trying to change the subject. Smart girl.

I shrug. "I hear there may be a cannonball contest later. Fable's judging."

This makes Bailey laugh. "Oh, you're going down," she says.

"No way. I've got the best cannonball in the game, remember?" I smirk.

I realize Lolli is grinning at us like a loon. I also realize that with Bailey by my side, life is so much sweeter.

• • •

Up next in this series is a book you do *not* want to miss! *Down and Dirty* is about the rookie Landon and the feisty Aubree. Landon is a swoony, stubborn waiting-for-the-right-girl hero you will melt for. There's plenty of high-heat first times and feel-good fun. Hang on to your panties, ladies! I. LOVE. THIS. BOOK!

DOWN AND DIRTY

Whoops.

Last night in Vegas is a blur. Now I'm waking up naked wrapped around Landon freaking Covington, my stupidly hot and younger guy friend, with a wedding ring on my finger and a marriage certificate on the table next to me.

Like I said, *Whoops*. I'm thirty. I should know better, but what happens in Vegas stays in Vegas, right?

Well, apparently not.

Because I've married the last alpha-male virgin on the planet. Yep, virgin. And my stubborn, oddly traditional new husband doesn't want a divorce. He wants *me*. But there's no way we could ever work. I'm a cat person. He loves dogs. I like tacos. He wants pizza. I love dirty, wild sex . . .

We also bicker nonstop about the dumbest stuff. The frown on his full mouth and tick in his jaw when he's angry are more than a little distracting. Turns out there's a fine line between love and hate, and crossing it lands me straight into his bed.

This is Book 5 in the Hot Jocks series. Each book is about a different player on a fictional ice hockey team, and each can be read as a complete standalone. Landon is a new rookie on the team. The heroine, Aubree, is the director of the team's charity organization. Enjoy!

BONUS SCENE

Asher

Suddenly it doesn't matter that we're in my teammate Landon's living room with him sleeping mere feet away. Because the second Bailey dropped to her knees between my feet, all common sense flew out the window and it was game-over for my libido. I've wanted her all night.

Bailey doesn't waste any time undoing the front of my pants or slipping her fingers beneath the elastic of my boxers to draw out my aching cock.

"Baby," I groan as she strokes me from base to tip. "You sure about this?"

With a tender kiss to the swollen head of my cock, Bailey gives an eager nod. "Very sure."

And with a look that says I want this in my mouth, Bailey gets to work.

I curl my hands into fists and watch, helpless, as my sexy as fuck girlfriend proceeds to give me the hottest b-job of my life.

Her right hand, curled around me, moves in time with her mouth. And her mouth… good God. It's hot and wet and the suction feels incredible.

A desperate noise escapes me and Bailey looks up, meeting my eyes with a look of warning.

"Sorry," I mouth.

With a deep inhale, I try to control my breathing, try to control the way my hips are lifting up off the couch to fuck her mouth, but I can't control anything. I can't last ... not like this. And after a few more pleasure-filled moments of Bailey sucking on me like a lolli-pop, I groan.

"Gonna come, baby."

She strokes and sucks until I erupt, swallowing me down like a damn pro.

I lean forward to kiss her forehead as Bailey grins up at me. "You're so, so good at that," I tell her. She chuckles.

A noise in the kitchen captures our attention. The faucet is running. What the hell? Quickly tucking myself back into my boxers, I help Bailey up off the floor.

"For the record, I didn't see anything," Landon says, waving a hand in our direction as he strolls from the kitchen back toward his bedroom.

"Thank fuck," I mutter under my breath.

"Well maybe I saw one little thing. Nice dick, Asher," he snickers.

Which sends Bailey into a fit of laughter.

I tug up my pants the rest of the way and rise to my feet. "We're leaving now," I say loudly to no one in particular.

Get Two Free books

Sign up for my newsletter and I'll automatically send you two free books.

www.kendallryanbooks.com/newsletter

Follow Kendall

Website

www.kendallryanbooks.com

Facebook

www.facebook.com/kendallryanbooks

Twitter

www.twitter.com/kendallryan1

Instagram

www.instagram.com/kendallryan1

Newsletter

www.kendallryanbooks.com/newsletter

About the Author

A *New York Times*, *Wall Street Journal*, and *USA TODAY* bestselling author of more than two dozen titles, Kendall Ryan has sold over two million books, and her books have been translated into several languages in countries around the world. Her books have also appeared on the *New York Times* and *USA TODAY* bestseller list more than three dozen times. Kendall has been featured in publications such as *USA TODAY*, *Newsweek*, and *In Touch Magazine*. She lives in Texas with her husband and two sons.

To be notified of new releases or sales, join Kendall's private Mailing List.

www.kendallryanbooks.com/newsletter

Get even more of the inside scoop when you join Kendall's private Facebook group, Kendall's Kinky Cuties:

www.facebook.com/groups/kendallskinkycuties

Other Books by Kendall Ryan

Unravel Me
Filthy Beautiful Lies Series
The Room Mate
The Play Mate
The House Mate
The Impact of You
Screwed
The Fix Up
Dirty Little Secret
xo, Zach
Baby Daddy
Tempting Little Tease
Bro Code
Love Machine
Flirting with Forever
Dear Jane
Finding Alexei
Boyfriend for Hire
The Two Week Arrangement
Seven Nights of Sin
Playing for Keeps
All the Way
Trying to Score

For a complete list of Kendall's books, visit:

www.kendallryanbooks.com/all-books/

CPSIA information can be obtained
at www.ICGtesting.com
Printed in the USA
LVHW090141120720
660314LV00014B/76

9 781733 672955